Some Sunny Day

Bruce & Heather:
Nobody can tickle
those piano keys
like Bruce can, but
our Dad gave it a
good try — as
you'll see when you
read this!
Best regards to
you both —
Tom

Some Sunny Day

Tom Douglas

Some Sunny Day

We'll meet again
Don't know where
Don't know when
But I know
We'll meet again
Some sunny day!

- Second World War
Inspirational Song

*To my father, for having the guts to stay in the game
Until he'd been dealt a winning hand.
And to my mother, for backing him all the way.*

INDEX

FOREWORD

The lung-searing sulfur fumes would roll in on the wind. Those who dared venture out of their clapboard shelters would have to tie a handkerchief over their mouths to prevent a fit of gagging and choking. Tears streaming down their faces, the hapless victims of this gas attack would dash from one spot to another, hurrying to do whatever had to be done.

In the distance could be heard the rumbling of heavy trucks carrying a fiery cargo that from time to time would spill down a hillside, searing the grass and turning trees into flaming torches.

As the sun came up, vaporizing the puddles of overnight rain, the sulphurous air would turn steamy and dank, inviting another onslaught of blackflies and mosquitoes that would leave everyone in their murderous path covered in bleeding sores.

If the supply train got through that morning, chances were that the bread was mouldy and the milk sour from sitting in an unrefrigerated boxcar while the crew strained to remove a rock slide or fallen tree from railroad tracks that provided a lifeline to the civilized south.

War zone? What war zone? This was a typical day in the small village of Sinterville in the wilds of iron ore mining country in the mid to late 1940s. The sulfur fumes belched out of a smokestack at the sintering plant where red-hot sinter clinkers were loaded onto huge trucks and then dumped down a hillside that once was covered with trees and grass and wildflowers.

Ironically, our family was sent off to this desolate outpost because my father had spent several years overseas, eventually suffering similar hardships – and much worse – on the battlefields of Europe once the Allied invasion forces had landed on the Normandy Beaches. Not knowing what to do with him upon his return, Dad's former employers had given him, his wife and two young sons a one-way ticket to the wild and wide-open mining town of Magpie Bay. Sinterville was a dormitory community of some twenty-three ramshackle houses just down the road.

How our family coped with, and eventually triumphed over, this unjust and insensitive five-year posting, my father's war-induced drinking problem and the deprivation of living in a settlement hacked out of bushland and quagmire is related here in a series of vignettes that provide an insight into a time and place that has been little documented.

Some of the names have been changed to protect the truly innocent and time has frayed my memory a bit when it comes to exact dates and numbers, but all the stories, with the odd embellishment for dramatic effect, are true. May they serve as a monument to the pioneering spirit of those hardy souls who opened up the northern mining areas of our vast country and as an inspiration to a generation struggling with the more sophisticated challenges of the new millennium.

CHAPTER ONE
Oedipus Wrecks A Homecoming

My brother Greg sold out for a pair of white boots.

He always did come cheap.

There we were in the clutches of a madman and all Greg could think about was looking good. I'd known he might not understand the danger we were in, but he'd sworn he did. He'd even crossed his heart. Twice. And hoped to die. Which was exactly what I expected to happen now that he'd gone over to the other side.

"Greg runs and hides whenever he sees me coming," The Murderer had said to our mother. "Tommy I can understand. He just glares at me. We were told to expect that. He's had you all to himself all the time I was away. But Greg seems terrified of me."

"Take him down to Megginson's and buy him a pair of white boots," our mother said. "He loves to get dressed up. He'll come around if you buy him the boots."

And the little traitor did. He came running back from the shoe store with a big grin on his face. Once inside the apartment, he made a beeline for our mother's bedroom where he climbed up on the chenille-covered double bed to look at his new boots in the long mirror on the wall. Then he *hugged* The Murderer.

I knew then that I was on my own. The other two had been fooled, but I wouldn't fall for any such bribery. Even if it was offered. It was only a matter of time, I figured, before The Murderer made his move. I had to be ready for him or all three of us would end up dead in our beds.

I could understand my brother Greg being tricked like that. After all, he was only two, while I was almost five years old. But our mother? Couldn't she see that this killer she'd let into our apartment was just waiting to attack us when we weren't expecting it? Hadn't she learned anything from all those scary movies she'd taken me to?

I'd smelled a rat the moment the man who was supposed to be my father stepped down from the train the day before The White Boots caper. My dad was a soldier. This man was wearing a funny brown suit with colored ribbons on his chest, but anybody could dress up like that. If he was really a soldier, where was his rifle? And why wasn't there a big brass band to meet him like there was for the other dads when they'd come home from the war a long time ago? How come we were the only people at the train station? Why wasn't somebody there to give him a medal? Where were all the people with flags and signs and those little rolls of colored paper that you threw around while everybody shouted: "Welcome home, Mel"?

I kept asking those questions and tugging at the hem of my mother's best dress but all she wanted to do was throw her arms around this ... this stranger ... and kiss him for the longest time and then cry. If she was really happy to see him, why was she crying? Was she keeping something from me? She'd never done that before.

He'd made his first mistake when he grabbed me up in his arms and tried to kiss me. This man definitely wasn't my father. He smelled like Uncle Harry did the Christmas he came to our apartment dressed like Santa Claus and read Greg and me a story, just before he fell into the Christmas tree. My dad hadn't smelled like that when he'd kissed me goodbye before going off to war. I was sure I would have remembered.

And this man wasn't anything like my dad when you took a really close look at him. Mother used to tell us that our Daddy smiled with his eyes. She'd say that again and again whenever we looked at the photo albums she kept by her bed. We used to do that a lot. Look at old photos I mean. But it wasn't the happiest of times. Mother always ended up hugging the album and crying. Especially after she got a letter telling her our Dad wouldn't be coming home yet because he had to help "de-mob" the other

14

soldiers. I didn't know what "de-mob" meant but it sounded pretty fishy to me.

This man didn't smile with his eyes. His eyes were narrow and mean looking. You kind of got the feeling he'd seen a lot of horrible things. I was puzzled for a while, but then I remembered. They were like the eyes of the murderer in one of the movies we'd seen, where a creepy guy came to live with an English family in their apartment and ended up killing them all in their beds.

Somehow this man, who was trying to make us believe he was our father, must've murdered our real father. Then he'd found out where we lived and had come to kill us all in our beds the first chance he got.

I'd decided not to let him know I was on to him because he might pull a knife or gun and rub us all out before we knew what hit us. It was better to keep my kisser shut and wait for the right moment to get the drop on him. That's what Sam Spade would have done.

After we'd come home from the train station. The Murderer must have slipped something into the champagne my mother had taken down from the closet shelf and put in the icebox before we left to meet the train.He tried to get my brother and me to drink some of it but I'd warned Greg that this man was out to kill us, so we didn't drink any. Well, I pretended to and Greg used up his one trick by saying: "I don't wanna!" and breaking into tears.

Greg got real ginger ale instead, but I decided not to drink anything because I had to keep my mind clear. I tried to warn our mother about her doctored drink by staring hard at her glass and shaking my head a little when she looked at me, but she didn't get it. She drank the whole thing in one swallow and did the same thing again when The Murderer refilled her glass and said: "Cheers, Baby." Before long she started giggling.

Laughing gas! I'd learned about that in one of the serials they used to play before the main feature. Laughing gas was a favorite trick of the creeps my real father had gone away to fight.

As I watched the champagne disappearing glass after glass, I thought about my real father and how this Murderer had killed him. My eyes got hot and the tears started to come, but when they asked me about it, I made up a story I knew they'd buy -- that I'd been reading too many comic books.

I had to be careful not to let the killer know I'd figured out his plans. I was sure that's how my real dad would have wanted me to handle it.

When the champagne bottle was empty, The Murderer gave our mother a funny look like he was trying to put her under his spell. It worked. She grinned and nodded and told Greg and me it was time for bed.

I knew for certain then that she'd been drugged, because it wasn't even dark out yet. The next clue was that she told us we could skip our baths just this once. Our mother would never act that way unless someone was controlling her mind. To her, godliness was next to cleanliness. That's what our next door neighbor used to say anyway.

And things got worse. As soon as we were tucked into bed, our mother and The Murderer went into her bedroom. And shut the door.

It took me a couple of minutes to get Greg to do what needed to be done. Since I'd already told him the man in the other room was a mad-dog killer, he wasn't exactly thrilled by the idea of knocking on the door and asking if he could sleep in the big bed like we both used to do. I tried to make him believe that our mother wouldn't let anything happen to him and when he still wouldn't go, I started reminding him about all the ghosts and goblins we had under our beds.

That did it. He began howling like he always did, ran out of the room and started banging on our mother's bedroom door, his thumb stuck in his mouth and his teddy bear under his arm. Before you knew it, the door opened, a hairy arm reached out and Greg and Teddy disappeared

The way I had it figured, The Murderer would let things settle down a bit and then begin by killing Greg. I had it all planned that when the screaming started I'd run into our mother's bedroom, rescue her and be out of there and at the police station before Greg had breathed his last gasp.

But things didn't go exactly as planned. When I woke up the next morning, Greg was sound asleep in the other bed and I could smell bacon frying. Well at least my little trick had delayed things.

It was after breakfast that our mother suggested the trip to the shoe store. While she and I were alone, I tried to bring up the subject about what terrible danger we were in, but she kept humming little tunes and smiling for no reason at all. Before I knew it, Greg was back with his new boots and I'd lost my chance to say anything.

However, I'd come up with another plan while they were away -- one that always worked in the movies. All I had to do was wait for the right moment.

My chance came once our mother had finished calming Greg down after he'd started jumping on the bed in his new boots and fell off, bumping his head. He was always bumping his head, or getting it bumped for him.

"Oh, by the way," I said in my best private eye voice, "I wrote a letter today and gave it to one of my friends."

The Murderer frowned at me but I pretended not to notice. Our mother was peeling apples for a pie and Greg was walking around in circles, looking at his new boots.

I had to wait for a few minutes because Greg wasn't watching where he was going and bumped into the open pantry door. It took even longer to get him to stop crying this time.

"As I was saying," I began again, "my friend, who shall remain nameless, has the letter I wrote. If anything happens to any of us, that letter goes straight to the police."

The Murderer and my mother exchanged glances. Couldn't she see the look of guilt that was written all over his face?

"Tommy has quite an imagination," The Murderer said, staring at me again. "Do you think we should have him checked out by a..."

"Of course he has a vivid imagination," my mother broke in. "He's seen every movie that's played in this town for the past three years. It was cheaper than leaving him with a babysitter. And he reads everything he can get his hands on. I started teaching him when he was three."

And that was the end of that.

But every once in a while I'd catch The Murderer frowning at me, and I knew he was starting to catch on that I had him pegged.

Days went by and nothing out of the ordinary happened, unless you count the fact that our mother seemed to be enjoying the new arrangements. I tried to tell Aunt Betty about the whole thing when she came to visit but she just smiled and patted me on the head and helped herself to another chocolate.

I continued to keep my guard up, carefully watching the man I now thought of as "The Murderer Among Us" -- a title I'd picked up at our grandparents' place from a True Crime magazine Gramma Hazel kept on her night table where she thought it was safe from prying eyes.

The day came, finally, when it looked like the killer was ready to make his move. He came home from a job interview looking as though he'd just been told he had to go back to war again. When he said we'd all be moving to some place that sounded like "Splinterville", the hair on the back of my neck started to rise.

But we got all excited when our mother greeted this news with the suggestion that we might as well move to the North Pole. Greg and I ran outside to tell all our friends we were going to live with Santa but before we could find anybody, we got called home for a family pow-wow.

When it was explained to us that we were actually moving to a place called Sinterville many miles north of Stackton on the Superior Railroad line, my alarm system let off more bells and whistles than the scratchy Spike Jones record I used to play over and over again until it got mysteriously broken.

The Murderer was planning the old throw-them-off-the-train trick. Thank goodness I'd seen so many gangster films. And, because I had, I'd be ready the first time the train pulled into a station while everyone else was asleep. I'd gently wake up our mother, put my hand over Greg's mouth to keep him quiet, and lead us all off the train and into the safe hands of the police. They'd finally get their man, thanks to me, and I'd probably have to go to the mayor's office to accept a medal or something. Maybe somebody would even make a movie about the whole thing.

I could hardly wait for the trip to begin.

CHAPTER TWO
Salute To Sinterville

Having his sons think of him as an evil imposter intent on mass murder must have been the final straw for my father.

He'd given up a promising position in the executive suite of the local steel mills to enlist in the army instead of waiting to be drafted. He'd been shipped overseas and saw his best friend blown to smithereens by a German mortar on the D-Day beaches. After a year of dodging shells, machinegun fire and sniper bullets from Normandy to Belgium to the Reichswald, he'd had a new kind of bombshell dropped on him.

Before the war, he'd been personal assistant to the general manager of the steel plant because he could type and take shorthand. These skills were soon discovered when he joined the army, and he'd become the Radar O'Reilly of his unit – seeing action and more than his share of carnage on a number of battlefronts. When the end of the war was in sight and everyone was looking forward to all the good things peace would bring, Dad's commanding officer informed him that his services were still needed to do all the paperwork necessary to "get the boys home".

Eight long months after "the boys" had gone home to a hero's welcome, my father stepped off the train in Stackton into the sub-zero temperatures of a January twilight in 1946.

There were no honor guards, cheering crowds or marching bands that bitterly cold day, only a wife and two small, suspicious sons. The war in Europe had ended the previous May and people wanted to put it behind them. A returning soldier was an unwelcome reminder of everything they wanted to forget.

The general indifference that greeted my father's homecoming hurt him deeply, but he did his best to shrug it off as simply another of the disappointments and indignities a soldier had to learn to accept. It was only when he'd had a few shots of whiskey that his bitterness bubbled to the surface. And those belts of rotgut occurred with dismaying regularity. He'd gone into the military a teetotaler but army life and the atrocities he'd witnessed on the field of battle had turned him into one of the walking wounded when hostilities ceased – an emotional basket case who managed to hold on to his sanity by anesthetizing himself whenever the heebie-jeebies hit.

His saving grace was that despite all the horrors of war he'd witnessed, he'd managed to keep his wry, self-deprecating sense of humor. On the rare occasions when he was persuaded to tell a few war stories, he invariably drew them from the funnier memories tucked away in his knapsack.

There was the time in Belgium, for instance, when he was sent up a dirt road to alert a nearby artillery battery with a conked-out field radio that they were shelling a house where Allied wounded had taken refuge in the basement. Puffballs of dirt kept flying up all around him but in the noise of battle he couldn't hear his mates shouting and figured the soil was being lifted off the dry ground by heavy raindrops. Only when he reached his destination did he learn that the plumes of dust were caused by machine gun bullets being fired at him from a Nazi gun emplacement in the upper part of the shelled building.

He never failed to get a laugh when he related how one of his buddies chug-a-lugged half a jug of what he thought was brandy confiscated from a German farmer, only to learn that he'd treated himself to a quart or so of castor oil.

A perennial favorite was the one about the time Dad had sung some crude lyrics to a Scottish ballad in an English beer hall and discovered too late that the drinker standing next to him at the bar was a six-and-a-half foot, sentimental and homesick Scottish soldier. "It's nae *Nelly Put Yer Belly Next To Mine And Wiggle Yer*

Bum," said the Jock. "It's *You've Never Smelt The Tangle Of The Isles.* Do you get that, boy-o?"

My father, dangling six inches off the floor at the end of the enraged Highlander's extended tree trunk of an arm, allowed as how he now knew the real lyrics and would forever after sing them properly. (He lied, of course. Nellie wiggled her bum in song every time Dad and his wartime cronies got together around the piano in our parlor right up until the year he died.)

These and other stories were fun to hear. But whenever Dad's drinking took him past the hail-fellow-well-met stage into the darker recesses of self-pity and acrimony, he would mutter a well-worn litany of remembered slights.

There was the long, cold train ride home to Stackton where, in actuality or merely in his imagination, the civilian passengers looked askance at this walking anachronism who was wearing a uniform that should have been stored away months before.

There was the insult endured at a stopover along the way. My father and some of his fellow Non-Commissioned Officers had been told to take their meals in the Officers' Mess because the Sergeants' Mess was closed for repairs. A beefy officer, whose meager collection of chest ribbons attested to a war spent entirely on the home front, upbraided the mess steward for not being able to supply him with a second piece of pie, then looked down his puffy red nose at the visiting Non-Coms and sniffed, "There used to be seconds before this riffraff arrived." Dad always maintained that his fellow NCOs restrained him from hitting the officer–and getting himself court-martialed – but we relegated that part of the tale to the "shoulda/coulda" after-the-fact revisionism practiced by war veterans, jilted lovers and weekend fishermen.

The theft of his kit bag, containing the souvenirs, personal belongings and small treasures that represented all his worldly goods from the war years, was another sore spot for Dad. Presumably it was lifted by a light-fingered railroad employee who'd slipped into an unguarded baggage car somewhere along the thousands of miles of railroad track that were taking Dad back to kith and kin.

But the final insult, the blow that had been delivered after he'd come home safely from war-torn Europe, was the one that caused the most pain.

When the executives of the Stackton steel mills -- most of whom had shed crocodile tears at having to stay behind to run the plant -- had promised all the brave lads who'd enlisted that there would be a job waiting for them when they returned from overseas, Dad hadn't noticed that the operative article was "*a*" job.

"Good to have you back, Mel, and of course we have a job for you!" they said when he reported for work, optimistic about the future and eager to start rebuilding his life. "What's that? You want your old job back? But that's impossible. Carson's been handling things ever so well since you, uh, since you left us and it wouldn't be fair to make him give it up after all these years, now would it?"

Carson, who'd been climbing the corporate ladder and making powerful friends while Dad was climbing down the netting into a D-Day landing craft to face powerful enemies, eventually made it all the way to Executive Vice President. Dad was made timekeeper at the Timberline Mine, the company's iron ore property in the hinterlands near Magpie Bay on the shores of Lake Superior.

And that's how my family ended up in Sinterville, a collection of twenty-three glorified shacks huddled up against an outcropping of the Pre-Cambrian Shield about 150 miles north of Stackton on the Superior Railroad Line. It was the cheapest housing in the Magpie Bay area and the money hadn't exactly been rolling in during the previous three years.

Whenever I mention the name Sinterville, people's faces take on a blank stare and they mutter: "Centerville? That sounds nice. Kind of homey." I usually agree, having long since given up trying to explain that the place got its name from the sintering plant that belched lung-burning sulfur fumes at us when the wind blew from the wrong direction.

"Sintering" was a procedure for extracting iron ore from rock. The material arrived by tram bucket from the Timberline Mine near Magpie Bay, a few miles away through impenetrable bush and swampland.

The buckets would dump the iron-laden rock into crushing machines that would pulverize it -- along with the occasional plant worker who happened to fall into the machinery -- and the small particles of gravel this produced would be dumped into a vat of chemicals.

By some magical process called "sink-float" that I never understood, the rock would sink to the bottom of the vat and the iron would float to the top where it was skimmed off. This sludge was roasted in gigantic ovens to liquefy the iron, which was then poured into moulds to form ingots when the brew cooled.

The ingots were shipped to the steel mills in Stackton by the same railroad that had delivered a disillusioned soldier, his heartsick wife and two kids under five years of age to this gulag.

The residue from the huge ovens, called slag, was transported to large slagheaps by gigantic vehicles referred to as Euclids -- which resembled oversized dump trucks on steroids.

The most popular kid in the area was the one whose father, a Euclid mechanic, patched up a discarded inner tube from one of those monoliths and let us all float on it when we went swimming at Magpie Lake.

The slagheaps towered into the sky and covered acres of the scrubland surrounding the sintering plant. On the night shift, the slag embers, just pulled from the furnace, would glow brightly and you could sit on a hill near the dump and watch the Euclids deliver their fiery cargo. I've never seen a live volcano in action, but I would imagine the molten lava looks a lot like the newly dumped slag that tumbled down the side of one of those heaps.

It was the slag dumping that finally spelled the end of Sinterville. The plant eventually ran out of space to dump their molten waste and so a corporate directive was issued to move the twenty-three houses out of Sinterville down the dirt road to Magpie Bay, about five miles away. If a house was too fragile to move, it was bulldozed flat and its inhabitants were left to find other accommodation wherever they could. The old boys who ran the mine didn't give a fig whether you had to live in a teepee as long as the work got done.

We left Magpie Bay ahead of the Great Sinterville Exodus and I've never been back, so I don't know if there's even a marker to commemorate the one-time existence of the tiny collection of huts known as Sinterville.

I kind of doubt it. So that's why I decided to set down a few memories about that time and place in an effort to prevent it all from slip-sliding away down a sinkhole of history without a trace.

CHAPTER THREE
Wild Goose Chase

The magpie looks like a crow wearing white underwear and it's reputed to steal small objects left around by unwary human beings. It was therefore kind of ironic that the small town my family was banished to was called Magpie Bay because my parents certainly felt as though something had been stolen from them – their future.

But for a five-year-old city kid suddenly dropped into the midst of a wide-open, wooden-sidewalked, mud wallow of a mining town, Magpie Bay offered a delicious peek at the kind of depravity the movies only hinted at.

The streets weren't paved with gold, but they were littered with drunken miners who always had a quarter to spare for an enterprising youngster ready to run down the street and fetch them a ham and cheese sandwich from Perkovich's Cafe or a pack of cigarettes from Hammond's Confectionery.

That quarter was your entry fee to Saturday afternoon at the movies. Well, movie, actually. They sent two up each week by train from Stackton. Usually there was a Western for the kids and a romantic comedy or thriller for the adults to watch Saturday night - - if the Lions Club Hall where the films were shown hadn't been left in ruins by the afternoon crowd of rampaging youngsters.

Backing up a bit, did I notice your eyebrows shoot up when I mentioned a five-year-old buying cigarettes for the miners too drunk or too preoccupied at one of the town's perpetual floating poker games to go for the fags themselves?

In the Magpie Bay of the late 1940s, if I could have taught my dog Tuffy to carry loose change and ask for the smokes by name, somebody would have sold them to him -- or anything else he had a fancy for.

That's why, after only a couple of days' stay at Perkovich's Hotel (Magpie Bay's commerce was monopolized by a very small group of entrepreneurs). I was greatly disappointed to learn that the Douglas Family would actually be taking up residence in Sinterville, a boring collection of ramshackle houses about five miles down the road.

If Magpie Bay, with its wild and wanton ways, was the 1940s answer to the Tombstone we used to see in all those Western movies, Sinterville was Buzzard Flats.

Sinterville's idea of a good time was to head down to Durrell's Gully come noon and watch the steam train negotiate the high trestle bridge over the Magpie River. At night, we'd all stare up at the Northern Lights and comment on how they got prettier with every sighting.

Not that it was all that bad for the average youngster. Within a stone's throw of your house, you could pick wild hazelnuts, blueberries, sugarplums, raspberries, strawberries and chokecherries. And, yes, I learned the hard way that it was only a stone's throw from my house. There's a special set of Murphy's Laws for kids, beginning with: "Any stone thrown randomly will always break a window."

There were death-defying hills to toboggan down in winter. And there were great stands of timber where you could while away those lazy summer days doing all sorts of risky things far from the watchful eyes of a worried mother or meddlesome little brother.

But my dad wasn't the only one to come out of the Second World War with an addiction. He'd fallen into the clutches of the demon rum. I was hooked on Hollywood. And I needed a steady supply of quarters to keep feeding my habit.

It had all started when my dad joined the army, leaving my mother and me at home in Stackton while he gallivanted all over the country getting his basic training. Then he was shipped overseas and it was almost two years before we saw him again.

In those pre-television days, my mother (soon to be OUR mother thanks to the little souvenir Dad left behind on his last leave before shipping out) whiled away the long, lonely hours between wartime shifts as a welder at the steel plant by taking in every film that played at Stackton's three movie houses.

Since youngsters, and babes in arms, were admitted free when accompanied by an adult, dragging us along instead of paying a babysitter meant money saved for her movie-going fund. And, having no one else to do a post-movie critique with, my mother would chat away to me about the relative merits of John Hodiak and Ray Milland or Virginia Mayo and Joan Bennett.

By the time I was five years old, I was considered the Walter Winchell of Stackton's Main Street neighborhood. I've been told that box office receipts at the nearby Strand Theater rose or fell depending on what one precocious little kid thought of their double feature.

Can you imagine my shock then when the reunited family was hustled off to Magpie Bay by the returned soldier's less-than-grateful employer and I learned that the town showed only one movie a week for kids, charging 25 cents for the privilege?

A new-found friend, much more worldly than I, assured me that the 25 cents was easy to come by. The town was full of miners every Friday night, pockets bulging and gullets parched. Once the good time gals and the dispensers of rotgut were through with them, there were still crumbs to be had as they raced each other to see who could go broke the fastest.

I never got a chance to test the theory. Within days, we were ensconced in our Sinterville shanty and although Magpie Bay was a mere five miles and a free bus ride away, no son of my mother's, to paraphrase her one and only discussion on the matter, was going to roll drunks in the streets of Magpie Bay and that was that.

Which left me with what seemed at the time like an insurmountable problem. Twenty-five cents was a king's ransom in those days and the only thing I had to ransom was a whiny little brother. I ran that one up the flagpole once and learned, much to my disgust, that as the older brother I would be held responsible for anything that happened to the little suck.

There was nothing left but to earn the price of admission. So I did -- learning very quickly that there were a hundred and one ways to come up with 25 big ones every week if you really had to.

The saggy old couch in our living room was always good for a few pennies and nickels after a weekend party at our house. But since it was considered communal property, I had to share anything I dredged up from under the cushions with brother Greg and, shortly thereafter, brother Norm.

There were all those wild berries to pick, but we usually ate as many as we gathered. This, combined with a couple of hours under a hot sun, gave us such a powerful thirst that we'd sell our pickings to the canny Sinterville housewives at a fraction of their worth and blow most of the profits at the Kool-Aid stand set up by Paula Jane Crocker.

Dew worm picking was another money maker but it was back-breaking work scouring neighborhood lawns with a flashlight late at night for the slimy critters. The going rate to the bait stores was four worms for a cent so this was a job you reserved for a desperate Friday night when you hadn't quite made enough throughout the week to earn your place on a hard bench in the Lions Club Hall Saturday afternoon.

There was the occasional penny to be made by finding a discarded beer bottle in a ditch or alleyway. Harold McHale, Sinterville's teenage precursor of Donald Trump, would take the bottles off your hands and save them up until he had ten or twelve cases, then ship them to the brewery in Stackton for a refund of two cents a bottle.

In winter, you could make a dime pitching in to shovel off the small rink where the miners and the millworkers battled each weekend to see who could break the most bones or remove the most teeth. But nobody at that time would have considered paying their own kids to shovel the walk, and since every household had at least one able-bodied youngster from whom to extract slave labor, there was no money to be made there.

I thought I'd hit the Mother Lode one Saturday after taking in a Western about a gunman who turns preacher. We had an old shed out behind our house and all it took was one nail and two pieces of wood to turn it into a cross-bearing church.

Jimmy Hall "borrowed" some hymnals from the real house of worship where his father worked as janitor, an upended orange crate draped with my mother's good tablecloth served as an altar and a couple of planks resting on chunks of firewood provided pews as comfortable as any I'd ever fidgeted on.

An old cowbell called the neighborhood to worship and the pre-publicity (Jimmy told his three mouthy sisters) must have worked because kids came running from far and wide to hear Reverend Thomas spread the good word. We were so ecumenical in our service that we even held confession -- with me telling professed bedwetter Madeline Hall to "go and pee no more".

The best part was when the service was over and the congregation had dispersed. The take was 76 cents. What an easy way to make a living!

But it was a short-lived career. I ended up being defrocked faster than a garter snake shedding its skin. Jimmy Hall was caught returning the hymnals and he ratted on our little set-up when the choir director kept insisting she'd caught him red-handed stealing the books. Imagine being threatened with eternal damnation for returning something. It doesn't seem fair somehow.

Anyway, my parents laid down the law that I was to return every last cent of the money I'd collected, even if it had been given voluntarily. And Madeline Hall swore she'd put in 17 cents when I'm positive she was the one who'd thrown a big red button into the collection plate.

Anyway, despite suffering reverses such as this, I still managed to come up with 25 cents each and every Saturday for as long as we lived in the Great White North.

I got so used to the deprivation of there being only one showing of one movie a week that I lost all sense of time and place the summer I was allowed to visit my paternal grandparents in Stackton.

For starters, the neighborhood theater only charged 11 cents admission and that got you previews, a cartoon and two full-length features -- which repeated all day long and well into the evening.

I remember my first day in the big city heading to the movies in time for the start of the show at 11 a.m. Then it's all a blur until about the fourth time the opening credits of a Rocky Lane western were rolling and I felt a hand on my right arm.

Looking up bleary-eyed into the flashlight of a uniformed usher, I stammered out a weak "Yes" when he asked me if I was Tommy Douglas.

"Well your grandmother says to get the hell home!" was his terse reply as he snapped off his flashlight and strutted back up the aisle.

As I raced home along the dimly lit evening streets of the city, I could hardly wait for this vacation to end so I could tell Brent McDonald and Gary James all about the night I was thrown out of the Orpheum Theater in Stackton.

I had the whole story firmly in place by the time I hit the bottom step up to my grandparents' front porch.

CHAPTER FOUR
Rocky Takes A Fall

You'll never know what being really miserable is until you've had to sit in an unheated outhouse in 40-below weather. And I'm talking Fahrenheit, where water freezes at thirty-two degrees above the zero mark..

When two Northerners meet in the depths of winter, they mumble through their lip hair: "Cold enuf fer ya?" If both of them are men, they might add an expletive or two.

I can remember as a kid waking up in the bedroom of our clapboard house in Sinterville with my hair frozen to the wall because the space heater in the living room, our only source of heat, had run out of oil overnight. On those days, it was almost a pleasure to climb into frigid clothing and make the five-mile trek on a wheezing, backfiring bus to our one-room schoolhouse in Magpie Bay. At least it would be warm there. Until you had to answer nature's call.

A town that existed to serve the steel industry, Magpie Bay had experienced something of a population boom during and immediately after the war years. This had created a problem of overcrowding at the one elementary school in the area.

Somebody got the bright idea of turning an old, tumbledown house nearby into a one-room annex but, through lack of funding or foresight, they didn't include indoor plumbing in their renovation plans. No problem. Over the weekend, they had someone throw up a two-hole outhouse. No insulation. No lighting. No running water. Just a box-like affair inside a shack.

And since little kids were considered to be dumber than bigger kids, it was the first two grades that inherited the annex and outhouse while the rest of the students continued to enjoy the relative comforts of indoor plumbing and temperatures that stayed in the 70-degree range.

The School Board, in its benevolence, passed a motion one particularly dark and stormy night that if the temperature dropped to minus 50 degrees, the schools would not open that day. Since Magpie Bay is virtually on the same line of latitude as the Siberian Lowlands, this used to happen fairly frequently from mid-December until the April thaw.

But oh those days when that stubborn thermometer hovered at minus 45 and you had to begin the ritual of dressing for the bone-chilling walk along that ice crystal gauntlet from your front door to the bus stop. Undershirt. Underpants. Longjohns. Two pairs of thick socks. Flannel sportshirt. Heavy flannel breeches we called "breeks" held up by elastic suspenders. A thick woolen sweater. Hockey toque pulled down over the forehead. Plaid woolen parka with fleece-trimmed hood. Mismatched plaid scarf over mouth and nose and tied behind the head. Two pairs of home-knitted mittens. Black rubber boots.

When the unheated bus discharged its cargo of frost-bitten zombies, Miss Grexton, our teacher, began the tedious ritual of peeling off the outer layers of Arctic survival gear so that we could take out our readers and learn all about Mother baking an apple pie for Dick and Jane and Baby Sally, who lived on a sunny street somewhere in Middle America.

Is it any wonder that as the big hand of the chipped enamel alarm clock on Miss Grexton's desk inched its way past 12 again and again, no human hands shot up seeking permission to leave the room? It was safer to sit rooted to the spot than to go through the contortions of getting dressed again for the elements. If an "accident" didn't happen as you struggled with the zipper on your parka, the shockwave of hitting that first blast of cold air outside the classroom could cause you to lose control of whichever internal organ you'd been clenching with all your might.

Miss Grexton kept soap and a washcloth plus a supply of non-descript underwear and unisex pantaloons at the back of the room where a hapless victim of equipment failure could clean up behind a curtained-off area. I can still see poor little Agnes Williams blubbering at her desk while a puddle slowly formed on the linoleum floor beneath her. Her fate would be to clean herself up as best she could behind the curtain, don the hideous garb the seniors called the "Oh-Oh Uniform" and sit in embarrassed numbness for the balance of the day while her clothes dried with a malodorous hiss on the space heater in the corner.

That sharp, distinct smell of soggy clothing drying as you sat in lepers' rags and, even worse, the taunts of your fellow pupils on the long, mortifying bus ride home were great deterrents against any of us allowing accidents of that sort to happen.

However, on the days when you'd slept late and had to wolf down your Cream of Wheat, giving your home bathroom a miss in order to make the bus, you'd arrive at school feeling like the condemned man on the day of his execution, knowing that it was only a matter of time before you had to take that long and fateful walk.

There are people who will tell you that the cry of a timber wolf is enough to strike fear in the heart of even the bravest of men. There are others who panic at the sight of a shark's fin knifing through the water. But to a little boy of six or seven in the days of primitive latrines, the thing that sent a shiver of cold terror racing through his veins was the jolt of awareness that the moment of fight or flight had arrived.

On those occasions, Miss Grexton, bless her heart, didn't stand on ceremony. Your mad dash for the door was excused and understood even though you hadn't raised your hand to ask for permission. With shouts of "We know where you're going" ringing in your ears, you headed straight for the little shack in the clearing, covering the distance in a hop, skip and jump that would have won a blue ribbon at the fall fair.

Once inside, you stripped down faster than a battle-weary soldier on an eight-hour Parisian furlough and hopped up onto the bum-numbing plank with the two circular holes cut in it. The only nice thing about having to go in winter was that the wood was frozen solid so you didn't come away with splinters like you did in September or June.

And you didn't dawdle. There's no greater incentive to getting things over with in a hurry than the knowledge that you're slowly freezing to death and you probably have about five minutes total before someone will have to come along and chip you off your perch.

But an even worse pitfall, in the truest sense of the word, of having to race to the "Jack Out Back" (as the seniors called it because it wasn't fancy enough to be referred to as a "John") was discovered one blustery afternoon by my friend and classmate Rocky Miron.

I was seated at my desk staring out the window at the whirling snow and mentally mushing my team of huskies to the nearest outpost with a bottle of life-saving medicine in a leather pouch slung over my shoulder. Suddenly, I became aware of every head in the room being turned my way and Miss Grexton standing there with a slight smile on her face, waiting for my reply.

"I was asking you, my little daydreamer, if you'd mind going to see what's keeping Rocky," she repeated. "He's been gone an awfully long time."

One of the drawbacks of being the teacher's pet, other than suffering the verbal slings and arrows of vicious teasing from jealous classmates, was that she often recruited you to take on a less-than-pleasant task. This time, for instance, it meant struggling into breeches, boots, jacket and toque and trudging through sub-zero weather to see why the kid who sat behind me hadn't returned from his solitary sojourn.

The thermometer outside our classroom window had been taking kamikaze dives into the minus 30-degree range every day since we'd returned to class from our Christmas holidays. A trip to the outhouse would have challenged Scott of the Antarctic and it seemed doubly cold to my six-year-old sensibilities since this particular trip wasn't one of personal necessity.

After a hazardous five-hour trek, that in reality lasted about thirty seconds, I reached the outpost, having had to shoot and eat all my sled dogs along the way. Well, okay, I actually polished off the remains of a peanut butter sandwich I'd found in my jacket pocket. I scrabbled the wooden door of the outhouse open with ice-numbed fingers and peered inside the unlit cubicle. Where Rocky should have been sitting in frigid misery, there were two empty "thrones". Too young to realize there was anything amiss, I let the spring-loaded door slam back into place and turned to run back to the welcoming warmth of the space-heatered classroom with the news that Rocky wasn't where he was supposed to be.

Luckily, the perpetually howling wind died down just then and I heard a faint, eerie call for help from inside the ice palace. Prying open the door once again, I tentatively called out: "Rocky?" and almost ran for cover when I was answered by a disembodied voice wailing: "Down here!"

"Down here" went beyond my worst nightmares. It was coming from the depths of the two-holer. Either Rocky was down there or I was about to be grabbed by an evil spirit that lived in outhouses and turned bad little boys into...

My curiosity out-wrestled my grisly imagination and I sidled up to the raised wooden box a drunken carpenter had nailed two toilet seats to. Peering down one of them, I could barely make out a moving object in the murky depths.

"Rocky, is that you?" I whispered. It didn't dawn on me until later that any goblin worth the name would have answered in the affirmative just to lure me closer.

"Yes, it's me. Get me out of here," was the less than cheerful reply.

The rest of the scenario is a bit of a blur. I remember running back into the classroom and announcing in a loud voice that caused Miss Grexton to suck in all of the room's available oxygen and clutch at her bosom: "Rocky's at the bottom of the shithouse!" I clapped a shocked hand over my mouth, but it was too late. I'd blurted out our schoolyard appellation for the outdoor privy in the heat of the moment.

But the urgency, not the language, of my message was apparently what mattered. I recall Miss Grexton running out in the snow in her laced-up high heeled oxfords to confirm my findings, then hightailing it across a drift-encrusted field to the nearest house at a pace that would have done Elroy "Crazy Legs" Hirsch proud.

Somebody found a ladder and, having raised the entire shelf topping the two-holer, climbed down to pluck a near-frozen Rocky out of the bottom of the pit. I braced myself for the outpouring of admiration that would surely come my way for what I'd done. I just hoped the senior boys would be careful when they hoisted me onto their shoulders. But for some strange reason, Rocky got all the attention and, after a while, it dawned on me that everybody must have sensed how embarrassed I'd have been by any show of appreciation.

A few days later, once his hero status had faded and Rocky had deigned to give us all the gory details of his journey to the center of the earth, I learned that a new Christmas sweater had caused the whole thing.

Holding off until the last possible moment, Rocky had finally answered the urgent call of nature by dashing out of the classroom clad only in the clothes he'd been wearing. He'd whipped off his sweater on the way to the latrine so that he could pull down the braces holding up his heavy woolen trousers just before he hopped up onto one of the two seats.

With more urgent matters on his mind, he'd absent-mindedly tossed the sweater to his left, only to realize in horror that it had dropped into the other hole. Terrified that his parents would punish him for losing his brand-new sweater, Rocky had squeezed down the hole and dropped knee-deep into half-frozen sludge. The befouled pullover was still clutched in his blue fingers when they hauled him out.

As still happens after an institutional near-tragedy, the powers that be resorted to overkill to prevent a recurrence of Rocky's fall from grace. From that day forward, trips to the outhouse were made in tandem. If Freddie Scafe had to go, Ronnie Berdusco was enlisted to ride shotgun on the trip. If Gwenny Haymes needed to be excused, Carol Carson acted as her lady-in-waiting. Rocky Miron and I spent the rest of the school year learning more than either of us wanted to know about each other's personal habits.

To this day, I can't help wondering whether the other graduates of Miss Grexton's Grade One and Two class of 1948 still check off a warm, solitary, lockable bathroom when they run down a mental list of their greatest blessings.

CHAPTER FIVE
The Walking Wounded

As a youngster, I had little chance to look up to my father. His wartime military stint, followed by his thankless posting to the northern wilderness, had left him with a monumental drinking problem.

Monumental drinking problem be damned. Let's face it. He was a drunk. He wasn't mean. He never beat us when he was on a binge. My brothers and I always had a roof over our heads, food in our bellies and clothing to wear. When Dad was sober, he was as kind, mild-mannered and gentlemanly as anyone on earth. But when "just one beer before supper" turned into three or four, we braced ourselves for what was to come. The pattern hardly ever varied.

First, he'd become sentimental. He'd sit at the piano and play tender love songs for our mother. Dorene -- or Dodie as he affectionately called her in that mellow period between the first sip of good cheer and that last, fateful swallow from Dr. Jekyll's test tube. "Near You" and "Kiss Me Once" would degenerate into half-forgotten war ditties that got more ribald with the downing of each beer. Eventually he'd succumb grudgingly to our mother's increasingly stern warnings to "stop that nonsense in front of the kids."

He'd retreat into the kitchen and we'd cringe at the sound of the cupboard door opening. That's where he kept his perpetual bottle of Old Porch Climber. A couple of belts of that whiskey while he grumbled at the kitchen table, becoming more and more incoherent, and then the snoring would begin that signaled his slide into oblivion.

We kids marveled at how he could sprawl unconscious on a kitchen chair without toppling over. We'd learned early on not to disturb him or try to get him to go to bed. While he never got physically violent, he could tear a young ego to shreds with vile insults that called into account every one of your shortcomings, including several you'd hoped nobody had noticed and a few you'd never even thought of yourself.

We'd leave him sitting there, occasionally muttering in his sleep as he revisited real and imagined slurs, and get ourselves ready for bed. Whenever we'd ask our mother what was wrong with Daddy, she'd tell us he'd had a hard day at the office or had heard some bad news. As the years passed, we figured he must have received more bad news than that Job character we learned about at Sunday school.

And those were the GOOD nights.

Sometimes he wouldn't come home at all. Our mother, or Maw as we started calling her after watching a Jesse James movie one Saturday afternoon, would start preparing supper around five o'clock so that everything would be out of the way in time for us to tune in to the evening radio programs beamed in from Stackton -- that long-lamented metropolis of 30,000 souls some 150 miles to the south of us in the land of civilization.

As each bus from the Timberline Mine, where Dad worked as timekeeper, trundled down our street without stopping in front of our house, Maw would become increasingly agitated. Neglected pots would boil over or she'd nick herself with a paring knife as she glanced more and more often at the ticking clock above the stove.

Even now, as I think back to those times, a feeling of cold dread creeps over me, starting in my fingers and toes and seeping slowly into the pit of my stomach. I have to consciously relax tense muscles and force myself to take long, deep breaths.

Supper on those fatherless evenings consisted of slightly burned comestibles served with empty cheerfulness on Maw's part as she tried to distract our questions by talking about the upcoming Christmas concert or school field day or whatever. Every once in a while she'd dab at her eyes and blow her nose, suggesting with a sheepish smile that another cold must be coming on, but she didn't fool anybody.

If it was wintertime, she'd have to put on Dad's parka and a pair of boots after clearing the supper dishes. Then it was out to the run-down shack behind the house to fill up and lug in a five-gallon can of fuel oil to keep the space heater in the living room from going out overnight. This was a job my brother Greg and I took over as soon as we were big enough to tag-team the metal container onto a toboggan, pull it to the porch and bump it up one step at a time to the back door.

I used to yearn for the sour smell of stale beer in the house the morning after one of Dad's absences. This meant that at least he'd made it home and was sleeping it off on the living room couch. Otherwise, he'd be gone for two or three days and the household would take on the chilled atmosphere of a death row vigil as we waited for some sign that he was alive and well.

Like many alcoholics, Dad was canny enough to time his binges in such a way that his job rarely came into jeopardy. Friday nights you could make book on the fact that he wouldn't be home. If he was still "AWOL" Monday morning, Maw would get word to his superiors that he was ailing. He usually had enough sense to come rolling in Monday evening so that he could make it to work Tuesday morning, hung over but able to coast through the day. Holiday weekends extended this routine by 24 hours.

I don't know for sure, but I suspect that the Powers-That-Were turned a blind eye to a lot of the drinking that went on in those post-war years because many of the employees were returned veterans. I'm not suggesting that this was an act of grateful compassion on the part of management. Rather, if they'd fired everyone who missed work because of a drinking problem, they'd have been forced to go down into the mines themselves. And it was easier to forgive the occasional indiscretion than to try to recruit people stupid or desperate enough to move to an area that had a widespread reputation as a mudhole infested with blackflies and mosquitoes where the highlight of the social season was the mine employees' five-pin bowling banquet.

I remember one incident during the period we later referred to as The Exodus That Never Was when we witnessed Dad run the gamut of crazed emotions from enraged madman to heartbroken swain.

My brothers and I were in bed asleep one night when we awoke with a start to the sound of shouting and pounding just outside our bedroom door. Sinterville's two-bedroom bungalows -- little more than insulated shacks -- were so small and cramped that one wag once suggested that if a mouse farted in the back shed you could tell by the pitch the particular rodent that had been indiscreet.

What we were hearing that scary, scary night were Dad's howls of drunken outrage as he banged on the door to the matrimonial bedroom next to our three-kid dormitory. He'd been missing in action for about 36 hours, which he considered no more serious than going to the corner store for cigarettes, and couldn't understand why Maw had barricaded herself in their bedroom.

When pounding with the side of his fist didn't do the job, Dad resorted to kicking in the bottom panel of the door with his feet. This brought all three of us kids out of our own room, shrieking for him to leave our mother alone.

Like an enraged grizzly, Dad turned his attentions from the splintered door and began a verbal assault on us -- using old army expressions that luckily we were too young to understand, let alone take offence at. But they were enough to bring Maw out of her sanctuary, and the sight of her stopped all four of us in mid-harangue.

A woman still in her late twenties, she was breathtakingly beautiful dressed in her Sunday best, her hair newly combed and fresh lipstick on her lips. The fact that it was about four o'clock in the morning threw all of us into a state of confusion, as did the realization that she had a suitcase clutched in her left hand while the fingers of her right hand slowly worked loose her wedding rings. These she threw at Dad while she shooed us kids back into our bedroom and slammed the door.

Dad stood dumfounded in the hallway while we followed Maw's hurried instructions to get dressed and to dump the remaining contents of our dresser drawers into the three suitcases she'd taken down from our closet shelf. Before any of us really knew what was happening, we were all standing in the living room, the silence so loud you could actually hear the slow whir of the second hand on the electric clock in the belly of the golden horse standing on the collapsed-leaf dining table over by the front window.

At that point, one of the strangest and most disconcerting things I've ever witnessed happened. Dad started to cry. Great choking sobs. Then he knelt down in front of our mother and begged her not to leave him. He blubbered all sorts of promises, gathering us three kids together as a kind of peace offering.

Before you knew it, all of us were crying -- and we kids were pleading with Maw not to leave Daddy. As the weeping and wailing reached a crescendo, Maw broke through the caterwauling with the promise that she'd stay for the time being if we'd all give her some peace and quiet by going to bed.

Dad repaired to the living room couch and we three kids stumbled back into our bedroom, climbing into bed and staring off into space until fatigue finally overtook us.

The next morning, Maw calmed our anxieties by telling us she and Dad had had a long talk and he'd promised to "get some help", which none of us understood. But the sight of the wedding rings back on Maw's left hand assured us that things had been patched up and that we weren't going to have to leave for parts unknown.

For a while, strange men came to the house to engage Dad in long, quiet discussions that we never got to hear because we were always told to go outside and play. He attended meetings on a fairly regular basis and weeks went by without any more incidents.

But Christmas came around and Dad allowed as how he could handle a drink or two without any problem. One or two at Christmas became three or four at New Year's and before long the old routine had begun once more.

But nothing as terrifyingly dramatic as that Living Room Ultimatum ever happened again.

And I never again saw my Dad cry -- until the day of my mother's funeral, almost four decades later.

CHAPTER SIX
Washed Up At Eight

Not many people can brag that they had a thriving business at six years of age. Nor that they engaged in bitter labor negotiations at the age of seven and won -- only to be washed up and penniless a short time later.

Well, it happened to me.

It was the dead of winter when our family arrived in Sinterville in 1946. By the time our brains had thawed, it was the fall of 1947 and I found myself in Grade One at a school in Magpie Bay, five miles and a bit down the road.

You see, Sinterville didn't have a school. It didn't, for that matter, have a store. It also didn't have any telephones. And the only person who owned a car had been tinkering with it, trying to get it to run, since the outbreak of the Second World War had made spare parts as hard to come by as canned kumquats.

The kids from Sinterville used to get to school aboard a decrepit old bus that wheezed its way between the village and Magpie Bay whenever somebody remembered to make the run. You could hear it coming for miles, so you had plenty of time to get out to the road. There were no assigned bus stops. You simply stood there and the driver figured out that you were waiting for a ride into town. Most of the time anyway.

It was that bus that provided me with the transportation link for my meteoric rise in the world of commerce. I'd like to claim credit for the idea that brought me untold riches, but in all honesty the scheme was too complicated for a six-year-old's intellect to have concocted. When it all happened, I wasn't that many months away from finally having mastered the art of tying my own shoelaces.

Actually, I owe the entire experience to Kay McCabe's hormones. Kay was in charge of the business before me but she had recently turned thirteen and had decided that making out after school with Jimmy Bishop up by the water tower north of the village was more fun than working.

It was the scandal of the week in Sinterville when it was revealed that Ken Richardson had fired Kay because she'd failed to perform her duties three times in a row. My mother poured tea and sympathy while Mrs. McCabe poured out her troubles at our kitchen table the day after the firing. Having done the neighborly thing, my mother allowed her practical side to prevail once a slightly mollified Mrs. McCabe had eaten the last butter tart and gone home.

Dressing me up in my finest overalls and giving my Alfalfa-like cowlick a quick combing, Maw hauled me out to the roadside and flagged down the next bus to Magpie Bay. One of her carefully hoarded dimes went into the fare box to pay for her ride. Kids traveled free.

My mother never ceased to amaze me. Normally a fairly shy and standoffish person, she would come to life like a she-bear with cubs when an opportunity or a dangerous situation crossed our family's path. On this particular occasion, she saw a chance to augment my father's meager take-home paycheck and there was no stopping her.

I don't remember many of the details after the bus had dropped us off in front of Richardson's Grocery Store and my mother had bearded the hapless Ken Richardson in his den. Well, to be more precise, she'd found him up on a ladder stocking one of his shelves and the poor man didn't have a prayer. By the time he had reluctantly agreed to give a six-year-old kid a chance, Magpie Bay's leading (and only) grocer was half-convinced that little Tommy Douglas was the next Abe Lincoln, Thomas Alva Edison and Horatio Alger all wrapped up in one.

To be honest, a trained chimpanzee could have done the job. What it consisted of was walking around to the twenty-three houses in Sinterville twice a week after school. Since I was barely able to print my own name, I would simply hand each housewife (that's what they were called in those pre-enlightened days) a pink pad of paper and a pencil. One after the other, they would write their name at the top of a page and fill in their grocery order. When I had visited all twenty-three houses, I would flag down the next bus and ride it into Magpie Bay. The accommodating drivers would usually wait while I dropped the stack of grocery orders off at the store and I'd be back in Sinterville in time for supper.

The next day, Ken Richardson would fill up the back of his pickup truck with the boxed orders and deliver them to the various Sinterville households that had requisitioned supplies.

It was the best job I've ever had. With no telephones or personal transportation available to them, the Sinterville housewives considered me a vital part of their domestic routine -- and rewarded me accordingly. Each of them seemed to try to outdo the next in seeing who could best fill my chubby little cheeks with exotic pastries and sugary confections. I became quite adept at sniffing the wind and anticipating Mrs. Docherty's shortbread cookies or Mrs. Lepak's apple strudel.

And I even got paid for it! On his second run of the week, Ken the Grocer would drop off my mother's order and reduce her bill by one dollar. I never saw the money, but at the end of a year, my folks ordered a brand-new bicycle from the Sears catalogue and I was the envy of every kid in Sinterville when it arrived at the train station. It was to be the only bike I ever owned and I rode it until it finally fell apart when I was fifteen years old.

Like all success stories, though, this one has a down side.

Everything had been going well for just over a year. Ken Richardson was happy with the job I was doing, the housewives thought I was adorable and I was quite content to continue shoveling in the calories while completing a chore that was easier than cleaning my room. Then Kay McCabe came back into the picture. She didn't want her old job back -- she was still having too much fun -- but she couldn't resist the chance to burst my bubble.

For reasons stated earlier, she was never home when I made my rounds. But one day I was later than usual and she was making her disheveled way up her walk as I left with her mother's grocery order.

"I hear Ken Richardson's paying you a dollar to take his orders," she smirked. "He used to pay me two."

I tearfully told my mother this distressing news once I'd made the return trip from Magpie Bay. She tried to brush off the whole thing by reminding me of my Sunday School lesson about the worker who was bitter that he'd agreed to work for a certain number of shekels and then found out that another worker had struck a better bargain. The parable hadn't made sense to me at the time and it still didn't. The knowledge that Kay McCabe had been paid twice as much as me festered away inside me for a whole week.

"Is that why you've been looking so glum lately?" said Grocer Richardson when I finally blurted out my displeasure. "Well, you've been doing such a fine job that I was thinking of giving you a raise anyway. Starting next week, I'll pay you two dollars too."

The victory made me giddy. I was too young to know much about labor negotiations, other than what I picked up from the disgruntled miners riding the bus at the end of their shifts, but here I'd just bargained a raise that had doubled my salary.

My euphoria, however, was to be short-lived. Before I could deliver the glad tidings to my family, I was met at the door by my exuberant mother who stopped me in my tracks with the news that my father had received a raise. We'd finally be able to afford the rent on a bigger house in Magpie Bay, which, after the deprivation of Sinterville was like moving from Shantytown to Snob Hill.

But even though I'd be moving five miles or so down the road, I could still keep my job, couldn't I? I could hop the bus after school and head for Sinterville, do the rounds and take the list back to the grocery store. This way I could just walk home from the store instead of facing another bus trip.

My mother hugged me to her bosom and told me what a little trouper I had been by helping out and all but it wouldn't be necessary any more. And besides, Wayne Walters, who lived next door to us, was a year older than me and his family really needed the money so she'd talked it over with his mother who was all excited about Wayne taking over. And it really should be someone from the village who did the job after all.

Like John L. Lewis bargaining with the coal barons, I argued my case, visions of sugar cookies with wings dancing in my head. It wouldn't be fair after a year of my sweating and straining twice a week, week in and week out for a year to build a rapport with the housewives and the grocer to hand over the job to someone else. This emotional outburst was accompanied by a thumping of the side of my fist into my open palm.

If THEY didn't need the money any more, I pointed out, they could give it to me. There were lots of things I could find to spend it on: sending away for an ant farm, buying a set of drums, saving up for a motorcycle...

Wayne Walters kept taking grocery orders for Ken Richardson until high school football practice started interfering. He eventually became a multi-millionaire in the mining industry and retired to the Bahamas while still a relatively young man.

I moved to Magpie Bay with my family and took up an endless search for a job as comparatively easy, enjoyable and rewarding as the one I'd left behind. That quest continues to this day.

I suppose there's a moral in this whole thing somewhere, but I'll be darned if I can figure out just exactly what it might be.

CHAPTER SEVEN
Ronnie Berdusco Owes Me A Hershey Bar

I was having trouble figuring out why Ronnie Berdusco hadn't fallen to the floor, kicking and screaming in agony from the poison that was eating away at his insides.

Instead, he was still standing beside me, a quizzical smile on his face and his open-mouth breathing sending wafts of garlic-scented chocolate my way.

The quizzical smile was the result of an unexpected gift he'd just received from an unbelievable source -- me. The garlic-scented chocolate was a combination of the heavily spiced spaghetti his mother had fed him for lunch and the candy bar I had so gallantly handed over to him a few minutes before. The only other thing I'd ever given him was chicken pox, so it was little wonder that he found my sudden generosity a bit hard to comprehend.

The fact was, I'd thought the confection was laced with poison and as the minutes ticked by without Ronnie doubling up in acute pain, I began to realize I'd been had. There was absolutely nothing wrong with the Hershey Bar that'd been given to me a short time before by a man I'd seen only once at a party at my parents' place.

Our house was Action Central almost every Friday and Saturday night. In post World War Two Magpie Bay, a piano player was worth his weight in beer caps. If he also owned the piano, his house became a weekend shrine to fallen comrades, half-suppressed war memories and the dawning realization among those assembled that the time spent fighting fascism had left them years behind those who'd been smart enough to avoid going overseas at all costs – be it by wearing a dress for the duration or finding a way to fake their physical.

I don't know about other houses, but at our place the kids were expected to behave like trained monkeys once the adults grew bored belting out the same war ditties they'd sung a thousand times or more. We were paraded in front of the company and expected to sing songs we'd learned by rote: "Bless This House". "Her Golden Hair Was Hangin' Down Her Back". "How Soon?". "Just A'Wearyin' For You" and other crowd pleasers my Dad pounded out on our cigarette-scarred, beer-stained, out-of-tune piano.

I wax nostalgic when I think of those songs now, but at the time it was terrifying to be trooped out in front of a bunch of inebriated strangers in our living room and told to perform. Nobody beat us if we didn't, but then nobody had to. We always sang our little hearts out because that was what was expected of us. Somewhere along the line it had been ingrained in us that you did what the grown-ups told you to do. Without question.

And that's how I found myself in the Lion's Club Hall one Saturday afternoon, hoping Ronnie would keel over just as the lights were turned off and the weekly installment of "Don Winslow Of The Navy" started to play, slightly out of sync, on the large screen set up at the front of the room. If my poison-laden pal swooned too soon, they'd probably cancel the one-time-only showing of the Saturday afternoon fare and find some excuse not to give us back our quarters.

There was no actual theater in Magpie Bay. Every Saturday, the Lion's Club put in rows of benches and screened whatever films had arrived the day before on the Superior Railroad freight and passenger train from Stackville.

Today's television-saturated boomers would find it hard to fathom a world without that medium to massage their fragile intellect. And it completely boggles their minds when you suggest that all Magpie Bay laid claim to electronically in the late 1940s was a single radio signal beamed from the civilized south. On blizzardy winter nights the reception would consist of radio voices sounding like penguins broadcasting a fish derby from Antarctica.

That's why the Saturday movies were a community event in Magpie Bay. The youngsters got their Saturday afternoon serial, cartoon and western and the adults could count on something a little more sophisticated in the evening when "Riders Of The Purple Sage" gave way to "The Dolly Sisters" or "Gaslight".

Not too many adults ever braved the mayhem of Saturday afternoon movies Magpie Bay style. There were dogfights -- nobody had ever passed a rule that you couldn't bring your pet in with you -- and every once in a while a whole row of excited youngsters would over-rock the long bench they were sharing and fly ass-over-gumboots into the row behind them.

I actually witnessed a scene once where the distraught Lion's Club member who'd volunteered to oversee the afternoon's proceedings got up in front of his raucous charges and announced that if one more dog peed on the screen all pets would be banned from future showings. He immediately disappeared beneath a hail of half-eaten cheese sandwiches, empty Dixie cups, candy bar wrappers, apple cores and orange peelings.

But sometimes there were family movies such as "Bambi" or "National Velvet" that played both the matinee and evening performances. Such was the case on this particular occasion when the fellow who'd been at my parents' soiree the night before called me over to where he was sitting and asked me to sing the song he'd heard me perform.

He was sitting with another man, who had not been at the Friday night gathering, and the family friend raved about what a great little singer I was. At that point, my discomfort at being asked to sing was in a tag-team match against my mother's warnings about not talking to strangers and my father's boozy insistence that you perform on command.

The proffered Hershey Bar did nothing to persuade me to burst forth in song. In the first place, candy bars had been in short supply during the war years and this was the first one of this kind I'd ever seen. And furthermore, I was convinced that this suspiciously friendly adult manufactured the contents and wrappers in some cobwebbed lab and used them to poison children. I have no idea why I thought this and my analyst is as perplexed as I am.

Finally, I decided that the quickest cut-and-run strategy would be to sing the song at top speed and light out for the other side of the hall, which to a seven-year-old's mind was like escaping to Australia.

Everything worked according to plan until I looked down and saw the Hershey Bar sticking out of my shirt pocket where my persistent benefactor had tucked it after my rapid rendition of "Mairsy Dotes".

Ronnie spotted the booty at the exact same moment and began hollering "Dibs" on his share of the prize. Certain that the first bite would result in instantaneous death, I allowed as how I wasn't hungry and handed over the brown-and-silver papered treat.

It disappeared in one gulp, paper and tinfoil flying through the air and settling around my companion's running-shoed feet. My deathwatch lasted through the screenings of Chapter Twelve of the serial, a Tom and Jerry cartoon and an entire Laurel and Hardy feature.

There were no death rattles from Ronnie. All I heard above the uneven soundtrack was the soft rasp of his mouth breathing and the occasional gurgle from his stomach as it merrily digested the unexpected sweetmeat.

When the afternoon's entertainment ended, my companion rubbed his eyes with his index knuckles, belched happily and said he'd see me at school on Monday.

From that day forward, I never spoke to Ronnie Berdusco again after the way he tricked me into giving him a perfectly good Hershey Bar and never even had the courtesy to offer me one bite!

CHAPTER EIGHT
The Night They Almost Blew Us
All To Kingdom Come

My dad wasn't one for doing chores around the house. Popping the cap off a beer with the Nazi belt buckle somebody had made into a bottle opener and dumping the occasional overflowing ashtray into the toilet, to his way of thinking, put him in line for the Helpful Hubby Of The Year award.

But when you lived in Sinterville, in the northern wilderness in the late 1940s, there was one duty you had to perform or you and your family froze to death.

The clapboard shacks some contractor with a sick sense of humor and the soul of a successful criminal lawyer had thrown up and called houses were each equipped with a living room space heater. These glorified steel drums guzzled fuel oil like a Russian-built tractor and had to be filled nightly to battle winter's 30-below zero temperatures.

All twenty-three of Sinterville's Yokum-like mansions had a shack out back containing a 50-gallon drum with a spigot on it from which you transferred oil into a five-gallon can used for filling the stove's ever-thirsty holding tank.

My dad hated the job and his litany of curses as he donned parka and galoshes to stagger out to the shed became a routine part of our pre-dinner table talk. On the nights when he was on a seventy-two-hour bender and didn't come home, the task fell to my mother and, later, to me and my brother Greg, even though we were barely old enough to heft the heavy can between us. To this day, I get sick to my stomach whenever I get a whiff of fuel oil.

Anyway, the 50-gallon drum needed frequent replenishing and this was done by a Frick and Frack team of oil deliverymen. They always managed to drive over a wayward toboggan or painstakingly crafted snowman in our back yard as part of the routine of filling the drum with a hose attachment they wheeled off their tank truck.

One particularly stark and gloomy night, Frick and Frack were late making their rounds and came screeching into our yard, knocking down my mother's fully-laden clothesline pole in their haste to make their last delivery and head for hearth and home --or, more likely, the beer parlor at Joe Perkovich's Lakeview Hotel.

Their job completed, they waved cheerily at my father as he walked to the shed, grinding the family's freshly-washed clothing under their truck wheels as they sped away.

Shivering and cursing as the wind blew a gust of air-borne snow down the neck of his jacket, my dad quickly filled the five-gallon can and carried it into the living room in preparation for filling the stove.

Exhausted from this Herculean labor, he struggled out of his jacket and cap and decided that before hoisting the can up to the gaping maw of the stove's holding tank, he would hoist a beer to his perennially parched lips.

That little gesture saved our lives.

By the time the beer had disappeared -- he was slow that night and it took more than thirty seconds -- my mother had dinner on the table and insisted we all sit down to eat while things were still hot.

Dad protested that he was just about to fill the stove, but it was empty bluster. He wanted to fill the stove about as much as he'd have welcomed the opportunity to mush a team of huskies cross-country to Mukluk Harbor for a temperance rally. And besides, my mother could be fairly firm when it came to getting the family to sit down together for a meal.

As usual, we buzz-sawed through the pot roast and side vegetables. Nothing whips up an appetite better than a howling wind shaking the house and threatening to hurl you out into the elements on an empty stomach. Greg and I were arguing with our younger brother Norm about whose turn it was to get the one maraschino cherry that had been placed in each can of fruit cocktail by a diabolical Libby's employee when a frantic knock sounded on our back door.

This brought the hubbub to an instant halt. Nobody in Sinterville made social calls on a winter's evening when the perpetual blizzard made walking more than ten feet in any one direction a major trek.

My mother and father glanced at each other as if the dreaded visit from the Gestapo had finally happened. Rising stealthily from his chair, my dad inched towards the door, which by now was threatening to fly off its hinges from the beating it was taking.

Shrugging resignedly, he flung the door open and was greeted by the huge bulk of Frick the Oilman, whose face was whiter than the snowflakes that clung to his fur cap.

"Oh my god, Mel," he blurted. "Am I ever glad to see you're still alive!"

Helping the distraught man to the chair he'd just vacated, my dad followed up by handing him his sure-fire cure for all of life's emergencies, a bottle of beer. After a couple of quick swallows, Frick explained that before making their last delivery to our house, he and his partner had offloaded 50 gallons of gasoline to a machine shop down the road.

In their hurry to get the day's work done, they'd forgotten to switch back to their truck's fuel oil tank and they'd filled our drum with straight gasoline.

"If we hadn't realized our mistake and turned around in time, you people would have all been blasted to Kingdom Come," Frick said with a weak chuckle that he quickly suppressed when he saw that no one else was getting the joke.

Now some men would have gotten angry and knocked the oilman off the chair for putting his family at such risk. But that wasn't my dad's style.

Having listened to Frick's plea not to complain to his boss or he and his partner would lose their jobs, Dad struck a bargain. There was no question that a new barrel of fuel oil would be delivered that night, no matter how long it took to get it there.

And since Frick and Frack had put us in harm's way, it was only fair, Dad allowed, that they prove when they delivered the new barrel that it contained fuel oil by filling our stove themselves.

In fact, he allowed as how he'd consider it right neighborly if they dropped by each night as they finished their rounds and filled the stove as a way of making amends for giving us such a fright.

With casually dropped threats, and a round or two of beer, my dad managed to string out this act of contrition that year until the first flock of wild geese had flown north over our house and the space heater had been shut down for a well-deserved, four-month layoff.

CHAPTER NINE
Where Have All The Soldiers Gone

He was introduced to us part way through the first term as Wolfgang. He eventually got over his terror at being amongst strangers in a confusing new homeland to the point where he could suggest shyly that we call him what his family called him: "Wolfie", which he pronounced "Vulfee".

I can see him in my mind's eye some fifty years later almost as clearly as the day Miss Yuzwa welcomed him to our Grade Three class in the Legion Hall that served as our makeshift schoolroom. And I still have a cracked and faded class photograph in which Wolfie, by year's end secure enough to let loose, is clowning around by waving at the camera.

But I can't for the life of me remember his last name. And I wish I could because I'd like to see if I could track him down and, if he's still alive, apologize to him for spoiling his first Christmas in his adopted country.

I didn't do it on purpose. It was one of those honest mistakes kids make and perhaps don't think about again for years, if ever. But there hasn't been a Christmas go by since I realized my cruel, if innocent, gaffe that I don't send a silent apology along the synapses of our collective consciousness, hoping that Wolfie will pick up the signal and understand.

Christmas in post World War Two Magpie Bay was like Christmas in Stalag 17 -- without the Red Cross parcels. Most of the inhabitants were impoverished war veterans and their families, newly arrived refugees or alcoholic hardrock miners with few ties to speak of. Money was tight and even if you had it to spend, the manufacturing plants had not yet retooled from wartime production to the peacetime spewing out of consumer goods that people would be willing to go into hock to buy.

My mother always managed to squirrel away enough from her household budget to buy cheap but thoughtful gifts for me and my two younger brothers. And, somehow or other, she also came up with enough to purchase something respectable for whatever classmate it fell to me to give a present to at our school Christmas party.

I don't remember whose name I drew that one particular year or what present I might have given, but knowing my mother, it had to be something nice. All I do remember is that Wolfie drew my name and that I wasn't exactly gracious in my acceptance of his gift.

I guess the first jolt of reality hit when Miss Yuzwa read my name off Wolfie's present and handed me a large kitchen matchbox like the ones my Dad used to keep handy to re-light the space heater in our living room when it chose to run out of fuel in the middle of a sub-zero Magpie Bay night.

Everyone else had received gifts wrapped up in Christmas paper, or at least in recycled tissue that Mr. Berdusco had used to cushion the kitchen ornaments he sold at his general store. My present was encased in a red, white and blue matchbox with my name scrawled boyishly on top with a dull pencil.

If time travel were possible, I would gladly fly back to that last school day before Christmas in the late 1940s and clap a hand over the mouth of the little boy who was my younger self just as I was about to say: "But these aren't even new!"

That would lift the burden, all these years later, of remembering the pained expression that replaced the expectant one on Wolfie's face and his hurt little voice replying: "I did not know you had to give something new!"

Crammed into the matchbox was a platoon of lead soldiers, their painted uniforms chipped, rifles snapped off at mid-barrel and several with heads or arms missing.

I draw a blank whenever I try to recall what happened after that. I'd like to think that I came to my senses and replied that they were just what I'd been hoping for. On a crasser note, I wish I'd had enough smarts to realize that these were pre-war German toy soldiers that Wolfie had brought with him from overseas and that they'd be worth a fortune at some point in the future.

But I have no idea what happened to the soldiers ... or to Wolfie for that matter. The story ends, in my mind at least, with that plaintive cry from a kid who had endured the horrors of wartime Germany, the indignities of getting settled into a new life in a new land and the disconcerting reality of having to make new friends and learn new lessons in a language as strange to him as German would have been to me if the fortunes of war had been reversed.

What bothers me most whenever I spin the memory wheel and the pointer comes to rest on that particular incident is that here was a youngster who'd decided to give up his prize possessions in the spirit of Christmas and ended up being rebuffed for doing so.

I hope the ensuing years have been as good to Wolfie as they've been to me. I pray that he soon got over the hurt and confusion caused by my childish insensitivity and that he today enjoys all the good things that life in his adopted homeland can give him.

And I console myself with the thought that perhaps he has somehow come to realize that my initial ingratitude was a fleeting thing and that I eventually became truly thankful for the best of all gifts -- the sharing of a personal treasure for all the right reasons.

CHAPTER TEN
Uncle Harry Flips His Wig

Being the oldest son in a family where the father had traded in his Second World War uniform and many of his paternal duties for a 20-year membership in the John Barleycorn Overachievers Club, I found a lot of responsibilities landing on my shoulders.

Some were less onerous than others. For instance, collecting the mail from the Magpie Bay general store that also served as the town post office was something to look forward to. The owner, a kindly man, always had some new confection he wanted you to sample to see if you thought it would be a big seller.

It was years before it finally dawned on me that he'd already bought the season's supply of the commodity and one small boy's opinion as to its marketability would have been not only much too little but far too late.

Anyway, among the Christmas cards and THIRD AND FINAL notices I picked up one early December day was a letter addressed in a familiar scrawl to Mrs. Dorene Douglas. Reading the envelope, I bit clean through the stem of the licorice pipe Mr. Hammond had asked me to test market. First of all, other than a baby bonus, I'd never seen any mail addressed to my mother before – at least, not since my father had come home. Secondly, I wondered why my rich Uncle Harry would be writing her a letter.

Well, he wasn't exactly my uncle, he was my great uncle, having married my dad's father's sister. But he wouldn't let any of us kids call him Great Uncle Harry. "When you weigh over 300 pounds," he'd say with a booming laugh, "you don't need to draw any unnecessary attention to it." Not that he was particularly fat. Several of Magpie Bay's hardrock miners had suggested so at one time or another and had wakened up wondering what freight train had hit them. He was big and he had a quick temper but he could also be the nicest man in the world, if you didn't cross him.

Years later, while surfing the channels on late-night TV, I came across an image of Burl Ives that gave me and the remote control device pause. The folk singer was playing Big Daddy to Elizabeth Taylor's Maggie in the Hollywood version of "Cat On A Hot Tin Roof". I sat mesmerized for the next hour or so because the relationship between those two was hauntingly reminiscent of the affectionate exchanges I'd witnessed time and again between my mother and Uncle Harry.

He openly adored her. A mountain of a man and bald as the proverbial billiard ball, he harbored no illusions about a strikingly pretty woman not yet 30 being romantically attracted to him. He simply liked her and got a kick out of her off-the-wall humor.

He called her "Sugar" and laughed uproariously at the zingers she'd fire at him whenever he and his wife came to call -- which wasn't often because they lived in Stackton, an exhausting ten-hour train ride away.

Uncle Harry was a big man in more ways than one. Realizing that our family of five was struggling to make ends meet on my father's meager salary as timekeeper at the Timberline Mine, Harry and his wife would ship a box of toys up to us every Christmas to augment the ring of gifts under the tree. Unfortunately, for all their generosity, they had terrible memories for names and genders. The year I was nine I got a musical top and my four-year-old brother got the set of Roy Rogers six-guns I'd been coveting.

That's how I recognized the handwriting on the envelope addressed to my mother. Uncle Harry was like a big kid at Christmas and took personal pride in addressing each of the gift labels himself -- much to our bewilderment when the present didn't suit the recipient. No one can ever imagine what persuasive powers it took for me to trade that musical top for my brother's six-guns. I made threats and broke promises that are probably chiseled in capital letters on some celestial scoreboard somewhere.

I held back the suspicious letter when I got home after school that day, handing over the rest of the packet and eyeballing my mother as though I were Philip Marlowe waiting for her to trip herself up. And she did.

"Is that all there was, Tommy?" she asked with concern after quickly flipping through the sheaf of envelopes several times. Mail delivery to Magpie Bay was erratic, especially at Christmas when the postal clerk got forgetful after making his round of commercial deliveries to merchants with a bottle of Yuletide cheer under their counters.

"That's all," I replied, then after a dramatic pause added with a flourish, "unless you were looking for ... this."

She snatched the envelope from my outstretched hand and tore it open, sighing with relief when two slips of paper, one white and one blue, fluttered to the floor. Before she could retrieve them, I scooped them both up, scanned them quickly and uttered something profound like: "Aha!"

The blue piece of paper was a check made out to my mother for the sum of $20, a sizeable amount in those days. The white notepaper contained one word in Uncle Harry's handwriting: "Shush!"

I had expected a guilty confession from the suspect. Perhaps a pleading request to keep this our secret. Or a quick admonition for me to mind my own business as she stuffed the incriminating evidence down the front of her blouse. What I hadn't anticipated was for her to burst out laughing and to comment about the accusing scowl on my face.

She was still erupting into snippets of mirth when my father came home from work a few minutes later and she showed him the mail that I'd brought home. Every bit of it -- including what I'd come to think of as Uncle Harry's extortion payment. For some reason, both parents had a good laugh when she explained how dramatically I'd handed over the one envelope.

Over dinner, while my younger brother drank his milk out of the Jungle Jim bamboo mug he'd received from our benefactor the previous Christmas when I'd been given a Snow White tea set, my dad explained that Uncle Harry sent my mother a check for $20 each year to buy herself something special. He got a big kick out of believing it was a secret shared between the two of them and, since money really was tight, my folks went along with it and no one got hurt in the process. The windfall went towards defraying the inevitable extra costs of Christmas.

Just how much my mother's opinion of him mattered to Harry was demonstrated one time when he and his wife made a rare trip up the Superior Railroad line to our little village. They took a taxi from the train station and my parents had only a minute or so from the time the cab stopped in front of our house until the guests were at the door to warn us not to say anything about Uncle Harry's new hairpiece.

Sure enough, he came through the door with a proud smile on his face and an elaborate wig on his previously bald head. One stern look from my dad was all it took to stifle any childish giggles that had been about to break forth.

The meal went off without a hitch, but Uncle Harry became increasingly agitated as no one mentioned the full head of hair perched on his dome. Finally, he couldn't stand it any longer.

"That was an excellent dinner, Sugar," he said, sipping from a glass of the wine he'd brought with him. "But tell me something. Do you notice anything different about me?"

"Yes I do, Harry," said my mother with a straight face as she began clearing the dishes away in preparation for dessert.

"Well, what do you think?" he asked expectantly.

Mother paused in the midst of retrieving a plate from the table and gave him a matter-of-fact look: "Do you really want to know?"

Uncle Harry's short fuse was legendary and I think my mother was having second thoughts about telling him the honest truth.

"Yes, I really want to know," he replied with a beatific smile. If a 300-pound ex-lumberjack can preen, he preened.

"Well, quite frankly," my mother said after a few seconds, "you look like Davy Crockett."

My aunt choked on the wine she was sipping. My dad slowly put down the dinner napkin he'd been using to dab at his lower lip. I think I actually felt the hair rise on the nape of my neck.

All eyes were on Uncle Harry.

Without missing a beat, he reached up, whipped off the wig and flipped it into a corner of the room.

"Well, Mel," he said, turning to my dad, "what do you think of those Red Wings? Aren't they having a great year? Do you think they'll beat the Rangers tomorrow night?"

There followed a communal sigh of relief and the involuntary tableau that had formed around the dinner table jerked back into real time. As always, Mother's dessert was a great success. Uncle Harry -- as special guest -- overruled my parents and let us kids feel grown up by having a little coffee in our milk. The singsong around the piano elevated gusto to new heights and three sleepy kids went to bed with a crisp one-dollar bill tucked into our pajama pockets.

The visitors had an early train to catch and were gone when we youngsters woke up the next morning. Like a posse closing in on Billy the Kid's hideout, we raced to the corner of the living room where Davy Crockett's coonskin had been hurled the night before.

It was gone -- and, to the best of my knowledge, Uncle Harry never wore, nor even mentioned, the hairpiece again.

CHAPTER ELEVEN
The Magic Of Christmas

Everyone who grew up believing in Santa Claus, the star in the East and the babe born in a manger has a favorite Christmas memory.

Perhaps it's the year that the weather and the transportation networks co-operated, allowing the entire family to get together in time to open their gifts and sit down at the dinner table for turkey and all the trimmings.

Or maybe it's the time Uncle Bill, fortified by a generous intake of eggnog, climbed onto the roof and hollered "Ho, ho, ho!" down the chimney -- sending a pack of wide-eyed kids scurrying for their beds.

Still others might remember with great fondness the Christmas Eve the snowflakes were at their fattest and laziest, the fire crackled on cue in the fireplace and the right person was snuggled up on the sofa sharing a hot apple cider and a kiss or two.

My favorite Christmas memory -- one I'll cherish for as long as there is breath enough in me to whistle "Silver Bells" --is an image of my mother standing on a snow-covered garbage dump.

My mother was the female counterpart of Peter Pan -- a little girl who never grew up. Christmas to her, even her last one, when she spent most of her time hiding just how sick she really was, meant poring over department store catalogues for weeks to make sure the perfect gift for everyone was on her ever-expanding list, practicing restraint by not putting the tree up before December 10, and fussing over grocery lists to make certain she had all the ingredients for everyone's favorite dish.

She once confessed that she was 12 years old before she stopped believing in Santa Claus. I think she was telling a little white lie. I don't think she ever stopped believing.

And so, back to that snow-covered garbage dump in Magpie Bay. It was December 24th and I was eight that year while my brothers were five and three. None of us remembers the incident personally, but it was confirmed to us time and again over the years by townsfolk who came to regard it as their own Gift of the Magi story.

My mother, as usual, had finished her catalogue Christmas shopping weeks early and the various gifts that had been shipped up north by rail from Stackton had been salted away in cardboard boxes in our back shed. Unfortunately, that ramshackle structure was also the storage area for the cartons and paper bags of trash that were collected whenever the town council could free up a dump truck to make the rounds.

As fate would have it, collection time that week was just before dusk on Christmas Eve. My father, who had gone off to war a half dozen years earlier as a teetotaler and returned with a drinking problem that took him a decade or more to conquer, was counting tipsy sheep on the living room sofa when the garbage truck arrived.

The driver, who considered himself a construction worker and not a "sanitary engineer", leaned heavily on the horn. This was the signal that if you wanted your garbage hauled away, you had better throw it on the back of the truck before he lost his patience and drove away.

My mother managed to rouse my father long enough for him to stagger to the back shed and grab hold of every box and bag in sight. His chore completed, he repaired to the sofa once again and continued his pastoral inventory.

As the story goes, my mother managed to bathe and bed down three excited youngsters after several readings of "The Night Before Christmas", then headed for the back shed to retrieve the long-hidden Christmas gifts and spread them under the tree.

What greeted her was beyond the Grinch's wildest dreams. There wasn't so much as a little toy drum left in the shed, all the stores were closed for the holidays and even if they'd been open, all the dollars lovingly hoarded over the past 11 months had gone to buy money orders made out to far-off catalogue stores.

Few people in post-war Magpie Bay had a telephone, let alone a car, so the teenaged daughter of our next door neighbor was pressed into service as babysitter and my mother set out on foot for a diner half a mile down the road where she knew she could use the telephone.

Once there, she called the local police station, a two-man outpost staffed at that time of night by Deputy Orrie Waito. He was there within minutes and drove my mother to the dump.

From her vantage point on one snow-covered pile of trash, she was able to spot that day's haul since it hadn't snowed in the previous 24 hours and the bags and boxes were heaped up where the dump truck had deposited them.

With the cruiser's headlights and Deputy Waito's flashlight illuminating the area, my mother began sorting bare-handedly through every container in sight. The truck driver had obviously cut a few corners in his haste to get home for Christmas Eve because there wasn't that much trash to search through. It soon became evident that our gifts were nowhere to be found.

My mother returned home in tears. Even her hitherto-unshakeable belief in the magic of Christmas had been dented by the events of the previous few hours. My father, waking up long enough to hear my mother's tale of woe, went back to sleep assuring her that Santa would take care of everything.

And Santa did. Within the hour, there was a knock on the door and Deputy Waito, an ear-to-ear smile on his beefy face, stood there with a large box containing all the gifts my mother had ordered from the catalogues.

Employing deductive reasoning that would have done old Sherlock proud, the policeman had gone back to the diner and quizzed the short-order cook as to who was within earshot when my mother had telephoned him. The cook remembered that one fellow had lit out of there like a singed reindeer and it turned out he had made a beeline for the town dump in his pick-up truck.

The only thing that shocked my ever-trusting mother more than the fact that someone would overhear her conversation and head out to scoop up our Christmas presents was that Deputy Waito might expect her to lay charges against the culprit. And at Christmastime, for heaven's sake!

And there was icing on the Christmas cake that year. One of Magpie Bay's leading merchants, Bernie Turcotte, heard about the plight of three youngsters who might not have any gifts under their Christmas tree. He went down to the dry goods store he had recently locked up for the holidays and grabbed toys, games and clothing off his shelves, showing up on our doorstep just after the now off-duty Deputy Waito had left with a couple of cups of bourbon-laced coffee under his belt.

"What the hell, I had so much fun collecting this stuff that I'm not going to take it back," Bernie said when he heard the news from my mother that our gifts had been recovered. "Let them have a double Christmas this year."

Little did any of them know that it would be a double Christmas every year from then on with the retelling of the story of how far people in a little snowbound northern village were willing to go to help Santa make his appointed rounds.

CHAPTER TWELVE
Flirtations In A Snowbank

All kids think their mothers look like movie stars. The difference in my case is that my mom did!

Picture a young Barbara Hale, who later played Della Street to Raymond Burr's Perry Mason. Now shade in a little sultriness à la Ava Gardner and you come close.

Add the zaniness of Lucille Ball and the irreverent wit of Carole Lombard and you'll understand why grown men used to make fools of themselves just to be around her. She'd kid them unmercifully and they'd lap it up.

I remember one of her victims who possessed a rather prominent nose. My mother had a different line for him every time he came to visit. "Hey, Pete," she'd say, "is that your nose or a banana you're eating?" Or: "Peter is the only man I know who can take a shower and smoke a cigarette at the same time." Or: "Here comes the world's fastest cherry picker. He hangs from the branch by his nose and picks with both hands."

Peter would laugh delightedly and come back for more. Again and again. He'd bring her candy and send her flowers and be the first to ask her to dance at the frequent social gatherings the people of Magpie Bay and Sinterville held to keep from going stir crazy in the northern bush.

My mother had a sixth sense for those who enjoyed her put-downs as well as for those who might be devastated by them. She never picked on anyone who couldn't take it and she never picked on anyone at all unless they fired the first salvo.

If she had one fault in this regard, it was that she wasn't able to differentiate between those who considered her attention harmless fun and those who took it to be a kind of offbeat flirtation. On more than one occasion, so the story goes, my long-suffering dad had to straighten out -- sometimes literally -- an overzealous, would-be playmate who mistook my mother's good-natured gibes for verbal love darts.

There was the time a Sinterville neighbor offered to drive my mother home from a party where my father was having too good a time singing ribald war songs with some new-found buddies. It was the middle of winter and much too far for her to walk home alone.

She accepted the ride, only to realize to her intense discomfort a few minutes later that the neighbor had just headed down a little-used mining road. To make matters worse, he kept repeating in a drunken slur how much he loved my mother and rejoicing at the fact that in just a few minutes they would be alone at last.

Alone was what my mother soon became as the car slid into a ditch and her enthusiastic admirer began snoring loudly with his forehead resting on the steering wheel. Anyone who has survived a northern winter will tell you that there is nothing more alone than sitting in a stalled car in the middle of nowhere with your fingers and toes beginning to freeze.

After pleading and poking got no response, my mother finally roused the sleeping Lothario by shoving several handfuls of snow down the neck of his shirt. She didn't know how to drive a car so she got out and pushed while her shivering suitor tried to rock the vehicle out of the ditch by gunning the motor at erratic intervals.

And that's the scene my father and Deputy Orrie Waito came upon a few minutes later as they drove up in the town's lone police cruiser. Someone at the party had reported seeing the laughing couple leave and my dad, whose feelings for my mother lurched from boozy indifference to intense jealousy at warp speed, headed for the cop shop to organize a two-man posse.

Once it had been established that my mother wasn't at home -- there were no telephones in the village so it meant driving there -- the search party proceeded down the few roads that were kept open in winter until they spotted tire tracks weaving from ditch to ditch and followed them.

Sad to relate, those were less than enlightened times and since the foiled philanderer was half Irish and half native North American, the Orrie suggested that he'd wait in the cruiser with my mother while my dad taught the "halfbreed" a lesson.

To my father's credit, he turned down the offer and the whole thing blew over. In fact, with a next-day apology from the abject neighbor, the story became a fixture on the party circuit that winter, eventually dying out along with the laughter.

Dying out, that is, except in the vivid memory of an eight-year-old kid who had a hiding place with a great view of our living room. On the nights when the parties were at our house, you could see things and hear things you'd never learn in a month of leafing through your grandmother's hidden stash of "True Confessions" magazines.

CHAPTER THIRTEEN
Doc MacTavish And the Six-Year Molar

My dad and I had our first beer together when I was six years old. A dozen years or so would pass before we got around to having the next one.

In addition to being too young to remember much, I was in a state of shock at the time, brought on by paroxysms of physical pain in my jaw. So my recollection of the incident has probably evolved more from family tellings of the story than actual recall on my part.

I do remember Dad trying to make me laugh by taking the glass of beer he'd just poured and blowing the foam into my face. Even at my tender age, I realized this was a clumsy but well-intentioned effort to distract me from my predicament. I remember thinking it was nice to be sitting there laughing with my dad and I tried a grin, but the movement caused another stab of pain in my lower mandible.

I can't recall the surroundings but I've been told our boys' night out took place at the staff house of the Timberline Mine on the outskirts of Magpie Bay. My father's job as timekeeper at the mine was a boring one, where the only perk was a key to the small house that middle management used as a lunchroom, rec center and dormitory on nights when their work kept them late.

There was a small refrigerator in the kitchen where you could buy bottled beverages on the honor system. After my ordeal, my dad took me over there and introduced me to his panacea for all of life's physical and emotional ills -- a bottle of beer. I don't think I drank much of it, but I remember the pain went away. That little seed planted in my formative mind would bear bitter fruit years later, but that's another story.

Anyway, the reason my dad found it necessary to try to dull the searing pain in my jaw was that I had just become the latest victim of Magpie Bay's shoddy medical system. No one in his right mind, least of all a professional man, would voluntarily set up practice in the raucous, blackfly-plagued, facility-deprived quagmire that the hardrock mining town of Magpie Bay had a well-earned reputation for being in the years following the Second World War.

Idle gossip, the town's second-largest yield of raw material, had it that Doc MacTavish had arrived one day by train in the late 1930s and holed up in the beverage room of the Lakeview Hotel for several weeks until he was satisfied nobody had followed him. No one ever learned what sort of medical misdeeds he might have perpetrated up to that point. Only those he was about to.

In a haphazard way that couldn't happen in today's mega-regulated society, Doc MacTavish eventually became Magpie Bay's only medical practitioner. And veterinarian. And dentist. Whether anyone ever asked him to produce credentials doesn't matter much anymore because he's been dead for close to fifty years. As have most of his patients, man and beast alike.

The majority of the inhabitants of Magpie Bay went to Doc MacTavish as a last resort. The owners of the mine provided him with a small clinic next door to the staff house, but he preferred to spend most of his waking hours in the beer parlor at The Lakeview. It was with great reluctance that anyone called him out of there to perform minor surgery that couldn't be done at his regular table in the beer parlor. Have you ever had a dislocated shoulder put back in its socket or a gash on your leg sewn up by a cranky, shaky doctor anxious to get back to his regular haunt before the head on his glass of beer dissipated?

And he was a better doctor than he was a dentist. My dad was once pressed into service as Doc MacTavish's assistant when the old fellow sprained his wrist (your guess is as good as mine) and couldn't pull teeth. I remember Dad, whose wrists were the strongest in town because he pounded a manual typewriter all day long, marveling over supper one night about how he'd followed Doc MacTavish's instructions and had yanked out a miner's tooth.

"Only he'd directed me to pull the wrong one," my father remarked, still shaken by the incident. "I thought the miner would pick me up and throw me through the nearest wall, but he just laughed and told me to make sure I got the right one on the next try."

So when I was stricken with a severe toothache one night, my folks tried all the home remedies: oil of cloves, cigarette smoke blown directly onto the tooth, a hot water bottle applied to the cheek. When nothing worked, it was decided that Doc MacTavish would have to be pressed into action.

My dad found the old gentleman picking pink and green spiders out of his beer glass, and persuaded him to take me up to the clinic to have the offending tooth removed. They say that, until the day the fixture was thrown on the scrap heap, you could still see the ridges where my six-year-old fingers had gripped the arms of the dentist chair in sheer agony.

"Oh, my god, Mel, I didn't realize it," the good doctor exclaimed to my father as the offending tooth finally parted from my jaw. "I thought it was a baby tooth. It's a six-year-molar that came in bad. I would've given the little guy freezing if I'd known that!"

Thus my trip to the staff house and my first sip of beer as my Dad tried to find a way to stifle my sobs of pain and his feelings of guilt for allowing Doctor Dipso to get his hands on me.

Next morning, I decided to get whatever mileage I could out of my war wound. Bursting into my Grade One classroom, I hooked my index finger into the corner of my mouth and proudly displayed the gap in my bottom row of teeth to Miss Grexton, the teacher I adored.

"So that's what all the commotion was about last night," she said, peering over rimless glasses. "They say you could hear the screaming all the way down to the lake."

You wouldn't think it would take much time to take your finger out of your mouth, make an about turn and walk sheepishly to your desk amidst the catcalls of fellow pupils. I'm sure, even to this day, that it took at least an hour.

I'd imagined Miss Grexton would have at least clucked her tongue, murmured: "There, there" and allowed as how I must have been a brave little man to go through such pain. One daydream on the bus to school that morning had even conjured up a scene of her laying my fevered brow on her bosom.

And I'd been sure that the wound was sufficient for Gwenny Haymes and Carol Carson to smile prettily through their tears at me while I manfully took my seat.

I'd envisioned Brent McDonald slapping me on the back at recess and saying with a stiff upper lip: "Well, done, old man. The boys and I have been thinking about asking you to join the club in our treehouse. We can use another brave member in our gang."

When none of these fantasies came to pass, I had to console myself with the fact that at least the treacherous molar had been worth five bucks to the tooth fairy – whose generosity seemed to match the guilt I saw in my father's eyes over the next couple of weeks every time he looked at me.

CHAPTER FOURTEEN
Greg's First Car

I guess I gained ownership of my brother Greg on February 15th, 1944. That was the day he was born and, since my dad was somewhere in England at the time training for the D-Day landings, everybody kept telling me I was the man of the house.

Apparently, that meant that at the age of three it was my responsibility -- as the little soldier it was constantly being suggested I was -- to burglar-proof our apartment, drive off any attackers who took a shine to my pretty and vulnerable mother and save us all from the bad Germans by always standing on guard. If I had any time left over, I was also supposed to look after my baby brother Greg.

My brother, by the way, doesn't to this day believe he's part of our family. A warped birds-and-bees story fed to him by his Grade Six health teacher left him with the impression that one's father wasn't one's father unless he was somewhere within a 50-mile radius of where you were born at the time you were born.

For that matter, Greg still believes babies materialize from under cabbage leaves, so I'm not surprised he's convinced he's the illegitimate son of our next-door neighbor who had chosen not to enlist in the Second World War. A goddam zombie was my dad's description of him.

Since the neighbor was a non-combatant in 1944, that meant that on the night of February 15th, he was probably in Stackton, where my mother was giving birth to her second son. And, since years later Greg saw the man kiss our mother under the mistletoe at a Christmas party, this was proof enough, within that particular branch of Gregorian logic, that the fellow was his natural father.

Baby ducks, I've been told, "imprint" the first living creature they see and thus believe they're looking at one of their parents.

Turkeys, it would seem, can take a rain check and decide years later who their real parent is.

Anyway, I spent close to three years being the man of the house and, whenever I could, looking after my baby brother Greg. The fact that we lost him when my chums and I took him out on Halloween as a two-year-old toddler wasn't my fault. When we asked him halfway along our route whether he could find his own way home, he swore he could.

And didn't I hold onto him until help arrived when an overflowing springtime ditch he'd fallen into was threatening to carry him away? I don't see how my having persuaded him to try to jump across the thing in the first place should at all take away from the heroic part I played in his rescue.

One of the things that used to annoy me about Greg was that he was always running. If he wasn't running to catch up to us older kids, he was running to "tell mommy" about some wicked thing I was in the midst of enjoying. Then there was the time he "ran for help" when a band of town bullies waylaid him and me in a dark laneway. How he expected to find help by scrunching down behind some wooden crates is beyond me.

I know I sound bothered. But that's how an older child is entitled to sound -- hard-done-by and deprived of the basic freedoms by some interloper who invades your territory just as you have it running smoothly.

But don't get me wrong. I love my brother. There are circumstances where I would definitely lay down my life for him. But as a little kid, he sure got on my nerves.

That's why I wonder sometimes whether I knew what I was doing when I left him as a three-year-old in an abandoned car with a bear grazing on blueberries a short spell away.

At the time, it seemed like an oversight. A bunch of us were down in the gully below our house in Sinterville picking blueberries and sugar plums in the hope that we'd get enough to persuade one of our mothers to bake us a pie.

Greg was happy because there was the burnt-out hulk of a Ford Roadster in the gully and he was merrily ur-ur-uring his way down an imaginary highway while the rest of us did the heavy work.

When I heard the first snort over to my left, I thought it was Amelia Lepak's sinuses acting up again. But after executing a double take the way Carl "Alfalfa" Switzer did in the Our Gang comedies, I realized that we were sharing our berry orchard with a gigantic black bear.

I cleverly dropped my berry pail, letting the clatter on the rocky ground warn my fellow pickers that I had decided to move on. By that time, I was halfway up the gully.

Not that I was the first one to reach the safety of our glassed-in porch. Molly McCabe, who had won the school blue ribbon for footraces three years in a row – and that was against the Grade Eight boys - had already filled my mother in on the entire scenario by the time I fell breathlessly through the open door of the verandah.

"Where's Greg?" my mother screamed. I remember thinking at the time that she might have shown a little more impartiality by asking after my health, seeing as how I was all tuckered out from my ordeal. However, once I got up, caught my breath and took a glance down the hill at the situation in the gully, I was more able to understand my mother's priorities.

Greg was still sitting in the abandoned car, twisting the steering wheel from side to side. The bear was happily munching away at a sugar plum bush. My mother was beside herself.

"Tommy, you get down there and save your baby brother," she yelled, all rationality having left her.

I'd give anything to be able to say that I made a mad dash for the gully, my mother hollering for me to come back, realizing how dangerous an order she'd given me. I'd love to be able to relate that

I whacked the bear on the nose, grabbed my brother out of the car and piggy-backed him to safety.

In actual fact, Harold McCabe, the senior member of our gang, had climbed a tree near the wrecked car when I'd sounded the alarm. He later claimed that he threw a dead branch at the bear. I saw the whole thing and what happened was that a branch broke under his weight and fell on the animal. At any rate, perhaps having had its fill of sugar plums, the bear wandered off and Harold and Greg came walking hand in hand back to a hero's welcome.

Greg got taken up in my mother's arms. Harold got a large slab of chocolate cake with vanilla ice cream. Even Molly went home with a bottle of my mother's nail polish that she'd expressed a liking for. There wasn't the slightest acknowledgement of the ankle I'd twisted while leading everyone, well, almost everyone, to safety.

To this day, I can't figure out what the fuss was all about anyway. It really wasn't that big a bear. More like a half-grown cub now that I think about it.

CHAPTER FIFTEEN
Playing With A Dead Fly

As the bus lurched up the hill, I told myself it would soon be over. I hadn't cried yet, and I was determined to hang on.

The incantation began again, louder than before: "Tommy got the stra-ap. Tommy got the stra-ap!" The cruel, childish cadence divided the dreaded word into two stinging syllables.

My palms still tingled from the half-dozen staccato swipes of the wooden ruler each had taken. My cheeks still tingled with the flush of embarrassment the incident had caused.

I was seven years of age and my whole world had come crashing in on me. Two of the three loves of my young life had betrayed me within minutes of each other. The emotional pain far outstripped the throbbing in my hands.

The wheezing relic that masqueraded as a school bus finally sagged to a merciful halt in front of my house. The chant grew louder as I walked the gauntlet from the rear of the vehicle to the front entrance. Brent McDonald stuck his foot out into the aisle, but I'd already learned that lesson the hard way and deftly stepped over the impromptu booby trap.

The driver, who had been watching me in the rearview mirror, yanked the handle that levered the double doors open and whispered: "Nice going, kid! You didn't shed a tear." as I stoically descended the short stairwell and stepped onto the gravel road.

The bus belched blue smoke as it trundled away. Several of its young riders tried to catch my attention by hanging halfway out the lowered side windows and yelling my name. I ignored them, staring straight ahead as I walked up our wooden front steps.

Once inside the sanctity of our front porch, I collapsed in a heap and began sobbing uncontrollably, hot tears welling up from miniature cauldrons that had been threatening to spill their contents for the past hour or so.

As I'd been counting on, my mother was there instantly, sweeping me up in her arms and clutching me to her bosom. At her gentle urging, I blurted out the horrible truth. "I-I-I got the-the strap," I stuttered moistly, the shame of it all sending me into further paroxysms of howls and snuffles.

A cool washcloth appeared like magic and I found myself being lulled into a familiar state of wellbeing as my mother told me I was home now and everything was okay. Her hypnotically soothing voice calmed me to the point where I could relate, between hiccups, the terrible afternoon I'd put in.

It had all started out so well. One of the two most-sought-after rewards for good behavior Miss Grexton meted out each day -- the other being wiping the blackboards clean -- was to stand on a chair at the front of our one-room schoolhouse and watch out the window for the bus that would take us Sinterville residents home from our day at school in Magpie Bay.

The bus would make its way down from the Timberline Mine and along Magpie Bay's main street past the school grounds. As the vehicle appeared at the left-hand side of the school window, this was the designated lookout's cue to shout: "There goes the bus!"

At that time, the Sinterville pupils would begin racing to the cloakroom to don whatever outer clothing the season dictated. Sometimes it would be no more than a light windbreaker, baseball cap and a pair of odiferous sneakers. And once the girls were ready, it was the boys' turn.

In the depths of winter, however, it meant hauling on heavy breeches, jacket, scarf, mittens and boots. Miss Grexton looked small and frail standing in front of the class, but she could wrestle ten youngsters into winter gear faster than a jumpmaster hustling a group of first-time paratroopers up to the hitch line.

By the time everyone was bundled up, the bus would have made its loop around Magpie Bay's downtown and would appear at the right side of the window. This prompted the litany: "Here she comes!" to be passed down from the observer to each would-be passenger in turn like a water bucket along a fire line. Everyone would then pile out the school doors to board the vehicle for the three-to-five mile ride to Sinterville.

Perhaps an aside is appropriate here. No accurate measurement of the distance from Magpie Bay to Sinterville exists to my knowledge. Nobody had a car in those days, the odometer on the school bus didn't work and the time I followed Miss Grexton's suggestion by asking the bus driver, he answered my question with a question of his own -- only his wasn't couched in the same gentle language that mine had been. Loosely translated, it indicated that he didn't know the answer and couldn't care less.

Anyway, to get back to the saga of Tommy's Terrible Tuesday. If, for some inexplicable reason, the lookout missed the bus's appearance at the left side of the window as it belched its way towards Magpie Bay's inner core, there was absolutely no way Miss Grexton could get everyone ready once the bus emerged on the right side of the window on its way to Sinterville. It was years before it dawned on me that if the old rattletrap had kept to some sort of schedule there would have been no need for a lookout and no embarrassing scenario such as I was about to experience.

After all this time, I still wake up in a cold sweat when I dream about the day I caused the whole Sinterville contingent to miss the bus. This indiscretion meant that we all had to wait for more than half an hour while the vehicle made its trek to Sinterville and back again.

I've been hammered in the guts, literally and figuratively, a number of times since then, but I don't think any of the incidents caused greater consternation than the horror of seeing the bus I was supposed to spot coming down the road from the left actually edging into my peripheral vision from the right.

When I blurted out the horrible truth, Miss Grexton folded her arms over her chest, a sure sign of her annoyance, and asked how this state of affairs could possibly have happened.

Before I could plead my innocence, Carol Carson, who had just that morning treacherously sworn her undying love for me at recess, volunteered the information that she had seen me playing with a dead fly on the window sill when I was supposed to be watching for the bus.

Miss Grexton, whom I worshiped, made it a double heartbreak by unceremoniously removing me from the chair I'd been standing on while looking out the window and replacing me as lookout with my arch-rival Brent McDonald who, of course, didn't fail at his appointed task of spotting the bus the next time it appeared from the left.

Having slunk back to my seat to await the return of the wayward Sinterville Streak, I vaguely heard Miss Grexton warning the now-unruly class that the next person to talk out of turn would receive a dozen whacks of her ever-present wooden ruler. No sooner had this threat been issued than the traitorous Carol whispered to me that I really should have been paying attention to my duties instead of playing with a dead fly.

Chivalrous to a fault, I tried to warn Carol in what I believed was a similar whisper that Miss Grexton had just said she'd strap the next person who broke the silence.

"Tommy, was that you I heard talking?" Miss Grexton snapped. "Come up to my desk this instant."

In mentally replaying the angst of the following few minutes, I always see a look of pained resignation on Miss Grexton's face as she delivers the coup de grâce to the tentatively outstretched hands of her pet pupil. In later life, I too have made sweeping threats to youngsters within my charge, only to be backed into a corner of no return when my favorite stepped across the verbal line I had drawn in the sand.

However, even if she regretted what she had to do, Miss Grexton broke a little boy's heart when she carried out a threat she had probably uttered in a moment of exasperation.

But Miss Grexton and Carol Carson taught me two valuable lessons that day that no doubt spared me a lot of grief in the years that followed.

First of all, never play with a dead fly when you're charged with an important responsibility.

And secondly, never ever believe a female who vows undying love when you're unwrapping a treasure trove of peanut butter and honey coated graham crackers at recess.

CHAPTER SIXTEEN
Hot Potato Boogie

Shirleen Witty tossed me a hot potato and I handed over my heart.

I had never before experienced such a tumble of sensations. The heady smell of steaming, succulent flesh. Skin black as coal dust and sizzling to the touch. A hiss of pent-up intensity at the first thrust of my probing fingers. The exquisite burst of exotic flavors as I took the soft, white, inner flesh into my mouth.

It sure beat the grease-coated home fries my mother served at almost every meal.

Some fellows remember, right down to the spearmint taste of her gum, the first time they ever kissed a girl. Others have fond memories of finally getting up enough nerve to hold hands at the roller rink.

I first fell seriously, head-over-heels in love the night Shirleen reached into the front pockets of her jeans and pulled out a potato in each hand.

Gathering up twigs, birchbark and small branches from beneath the trees hiding us from the rest of humanity, she next produced a kitchen match from her pocket, scraped it against a nearby rock and soon had a small bonfire blazing.

At seven years of age, I wasn't even allowed to touch the cardboard matchbox my dad kept next to the space heater in our living room, let alone take a match from it. A frisson of unfamiliar depravity coursed through me as a realized I was in the company of a girl who really knew her way around.

Even more enthralling, she had to be at least ten years old, a member of that "wild" Witty family that lived just outside of town and was always getting into some sort of trouble that kept tongues wagging from one end of Magpie Bay to the other.

What had I done to fall into the clutches of this older woman? Well, for starters, I was the only one in our group to answer "I would" when she asked who'd like to go out in the bush and play pioneer. I didn't know what a pioneer was, but it had to be more fun than catching lightning bugs in a Mason jar, which was what I'd been doing with my brother Greg and a couple of other guys when Shirleen wandered by.

With Greg's whiny voice ringing in my ears that he was going to tell Mommy, Shirleen and I headed for the stand of timber out behind our house while my erstwhile companions raced home to spread the news of my wicked downfall. I might end up getting whacked with the big stick my mother kept handy to hoist clothes out of the boiling water in her ancient washing machine, but something told me it would be worth it.

And it was. Over the years, I have dined on baked potatoes smothered in sour cream and sprinkled with caviar in the Queen's Grill of the luxurious Queen Elizabeth 2 as the mighty ocean liner plied its way to Europe across the North Atlantic. I have savored that first, crunchy bite of *patate frite* in a Parisian brasserie. I have gorged myself on the tangy *kartofflen* they serve with sauerkraut and sausage at the Munich Oktoberfest.

But I have never tasted anything as mouthwateringly memorable as that charcoal-blistered potato Shirleen served me on a stick in the wilds of Magpie Bay that summer night almost fifty years ago.

No salt and pepper. No butter. No fancy foil jacket. Just an ash-covered tuber that she'd tossed into the fire and we'd waited for while we scratched our blackfly bites and talked about the Wild Bill Elliot movie we'd seen the Saturday before at the Lion's Club Hall.

A girl who liked Wild Bill Elliot and could cook like she could? I was sure I'd found my life's companion.

But it wasn't to be. Perhaps I committed some unpardonable *faux pas* by letting her stomp out the embers of our makeshift campfire all by herself while I gnawed at the last morsel of my first *pomme de terre au grit.* Or maybe I broke some law of the frontier by cutting short our stint as pioneers, allowing as how it was getting dark and I had to get home before I got a real licking.

Anyway, from that day forward, despite several clumsy attempts on my part to entice Shirleen back into the woods in a futile effort to recapture that one magic night, I didn't seem to exist any more when she was around. Gary James, who was a couple of years older than me, whispered to a gaggle of his friends that he'd played pioneer with Shirleen and the story session broke up with dirty little-boy snickers and mocking glances in my direction.

I think the whole thing ran its course in a week or so and that would have been the end of it except for the fact that fate had one more dirty trick to play on me.

The following Friday night, my mother and dad were preparing to stroll down the street to the McCabes' place where they enjoyed a weekly round-robin Cribbage tournament. Even though I was seven going on eight, my parents still insisted that one of the older neighborhood kids stay with us for the couple of hours they'd be out socializing.

"That must be the new babysitter now," my mother called from her bedroom as she touched up her lipstick. "Would you please let her in, Tommy?"

When I replay the scene on my mental VCR, I endow the Tommy Douglas of those days with a strong feeling of premonition as though sensing that something was about to happen that would come as a real shock.

But that's probably been added in the editing room because I can't think of any signs that would have given me warning. New babysitters were common at our house. We went through them like chunks of ice from the blockhouse on a hot summer's day.

At any rate, I did my mother's bidding and, to paraphrase an old expression: Love flew out the window the minute Shirleen Witty walked through the door.

CHAPTER SEVENTEEN
The Harper Touch

Her face haunts me to this day.

Melody Harper.

Eyes as flat and expressionless as the roadkill you couldn't help looking at when you were trying to hitch a ride from Sinterville to Magpie Bay for a swim on a hot summer day.

A mouth as set and stern as those you see in old photographs of pioneer women slumped wearily outside their sod huts.

An emaciated body clad in hand-me-downs that looked as though they hadn't been within spitting distance of soap and water in recent memory.

And a head of hair that very likely served as the tangled home of more than one species of six-legged critters.

It was the year we younger kids "graduated" from the clapboard one-room school to the large, squat institutionalized building down the road. That made it Grade 3, so I was about eight years old at the time. She was in Grade 7 or 8 and must have been around 12, although she had a weary resignation to her that put her well beyond her years.

Melody Harper. What kind of magnificent plans had someone had for a new-born infant pretty enough to be named Melody? Were there music lessons in the offing? Or ballet? Did the name-giver hope the little girl would grow up to be a famous actress? A country-and-western singer perhaps.

Anyway, things didn't go according to plan, at least for the short while that Melody and I shared time and space together. In the caste system that existed in any schoolyard I ever played in, Melody was a leper. She was one of "those Harper people" who lived in a tarpaper shack out in the woods somewhere. She and half a dozen brothers and sisters attended our school, but none of them said very much.

In fact, you couldn't even get a rise out of them when you brushed up against one of them and then placed your hand on the next person you met, whispering ominously: "You've got The Harper Touch!"

This ritual would cause the "infected" party to shudder, swipe a hand over the part of his or her body contaminated in such a vile way and race to the next victim, offloading The Harper Touch and whispering the curse.

If the mean streak was wide enough in the collection of vile little creatures standing around the schoolyard when the game got started, it could last all the way through recess.

To my everlasting regret, I have to admit that I played the game. At the time, it seemed like innocent fun. Nobody actually got harmed by it and besides, you were afraid that if you didn't play, the rules would be changed and people would start cringing away from being infected with something revolting that bore your name.

Talk about children's playgrounds being microcosms of global societies. At that time, we were little more than a decade and an ocean removed from Kristalnacht and jackboots and The Final Solution.

But we were only kids, the apologist within me insists. We didn't really know that we were hurting anyone's feelings. And yet I can still see all the Harpers running to one end of the schoolyard when the game began, the younger ones huddling behind the older ones, who stood outward like musk oxen defending their herd against predators.

As usual, The Game was played right under the noses of the teachers who were supposed to be supervising us, without them being aware of what was going on. The kids were playing tag and that kept them out of trouble, so don't upset the apple cart seemed to be the order of the day.

The inevitable, however, finally happened. During that restless, volatile last week before summer holidays, the youngest -- and thus the least hardened -- Harper, a little girl in Grade One, broke into tears at the razzing she was taking one day. The newest -- and thus the least hardened -- teacher heard her tale of woe with increasing outrage.

The matter must have been discussed at a hurried staff meeting because orders came down from on high -- The Principal's Office -- that the next person who uttered the curse would be called up in front of the entire school and given the strap -- a long strip of rubberized canvas the principal always carried with him in his back pocket.

Like so many acts of legislation that are passed to punish the guilty and end up damaging the innocent, the principal's edict backfired. Unfortunately he, being the jerk he was, rigidly stuck to the rule rather than finding a graceful way out.

What happened was that Melody Harper, responding to whatever demons had been eating away at her throughout the eight years she'd attended the school, chose the hushed moment just before the principal declared the school closed for the summer holidays to make her stand.

Like Ike addressing his troops before Operation Overlord, our fatuous principal had lined us all up in the schoolyard, row upon row, where he could make his farewell address to a captive audience.

He'd just finished and was taking in a deep breath to make his long-awaited announcement when Melody reached out to the girl in the next row and in a stage whisper that could be heard from one end of the schoolyard to the other announced: "You've got The Harper Touch."

A smart man would have ignored the remark, quickly announce year's end and let the incident lie trampled in the dust raised by sixty excited youngsters heading for the hills.

But our principal was not a smart man. "Who said that?" he barked, then blanched when Melody disdainfully raised the offending hand.

I wish I were making this all up, but anyone who was there that day will confirm that Magpie Bay's answer to Ichabod Crane called Melody to the front of the assembly, muttered something about rules being rules, and administered several teeth-clenching blows of the "Black Doctor" as he so cutely referred to his strap whenever he pulled it out to threaten the inmates. Even then we knew there was something sick about the way he fondled the thing.

I still remember, with admiration and a certain amount of self-recrimination, what the disdainfully cool and collected Melody muttered in a loud aside as she ambled slowly back to her place in line that day: "Now HE'S got The Harper Touch."

Either not hearing or choosing to ignore that remark, the principal turned embarrassed silence into pandemonium by announcing the holiday.

That summer, our family moved from Magpie Bay and I never saw or heard about Melody again. But I think of her from time to time, always with the fervent hope that The Harper Touch turned out to have magical properties that somewhere, somehow turned her life into a beautiful song.

CHAPTER EIGHTEEN
Lest We Forget

The first time it happened, I thought a banshee from hell had landed on my bedroom windowsill and was screeching to his packmates that they'd finally tracked me down.

Well, what would you expect of a seven-year-old with a vivid imagination who'd just been wakened from a sound sleep by the strangest racket imaginable?

This was my introduction to a ritual that from then on marked an annual event most people consider a solemn occasion -- the November 11th honoring of those who have died while in the service of their country.

The noise by which I had been so rudely awakened was the squawk of a set of bagpipes on our lawn. The piper, who'd served in the British Army during the Second World War, had obviously lubricated more than his chanter in preparing for his yearly call-to-battle or lament for the fallen or whatever it was he was trying to blast through the wheezy instrument he carried under his arm.

As I peeked out the window, I caught a glimpse of a struggling face, purple-hued and covered by a sheen of sweat. He looked like a Shriner at a community picnic trying to blow up balloons after a night of riding his little motorcycle up and down hotel corridors.

The fact that he was probably freezing to death couldn't have made his task any easier. Seven o'clock in the morning on November 11th in Sinterville, especially if you weren't wearing any knickers under your kilt, would have been a daunting experience for the hardiest of men -- which this one definitely did not appear to be.

As my father bustled around in the kitchen, getting out cups and a bottle of whiskey, he kept badgering my mother to get the coffee going. Dad had never mastered the art of cooking.

The piper traipsed across the kitchen, trailing mud and wet grass behind him. Then he sheepishly retraced his steps, removed his brogans and swabbed up the mess with the mop my mother had handed him. She'd make their coffee, but she wouldn't clean up after them.

His pipes groaning thankfully as they were laid to rest in a corner, the piper -- Angus McSporran or whatever his name was -- thanked my father for the proffered "Heart Starter" in an accent so thick you could cut butterscotch with it. He then declined my mother's offer of breakfast in a soft croon that would have charmed the dew off the heather.

The neighbors had just had time to go back to sleep when the air was rent again, this time by a number of short blasts on a cacophony of car horns as the Sinterville and Magpie Bay Brigade of the local veterans' association wheezed up to our front door in whatever vehicles they had been able to commandeer for the occasion. There were, amongst others, a steam-belching old school bus, a contractor's dilapidated pickup, a battle-weary Jeep and the Mudge Mongrel -- a car Louie Mudge, local amateur mechanic, had cannibalized from the wrecks abandoned in fields throughout the area.

What I was witnessing was the first of a series of rituals that would take place at our house every November 11th, June 6th (D-Day) and the anniversary of every other battle "The Old Farts", as they called themselves, had ever fought in or even read about. My father didn't have a barn, but he had a piano, a repertoire of war songs and romantic ballads and a couple of kids he'd taught to march into the living room at a given signal, wooden rifles on our shoulders, singing such crowd-pleasers as "Old Soldiers Never Die" and "Now Is The Hour".

From our point of view, these events were quite lucrative once you got over your initial terror. After we finished our songs, there wouldn't be a dry eye in the house and we'd find our pockets being stuffed with silver and even folding money. Our parents would siphon off a fair amount of our take in the days ahead when they ran out of cash for cigarettes and a few staples like milk and bread, but there was usually enough left over to pay for a Saturday afternoon movie or two and a bag of licorice jawbreakers and soft caramels.

In fact, the assaults on Fort Douglas would have been fun if the revelers had known when to quit. But the 11 o'clock Veterans Parade and Ceremony plus the obligatory afternoon at the Legion Hall swapping jugs of draft beer and kitbags of war memories were only necessary interruptions in the all-day party at our house.

Late in the afternoon, the piper would be back on our lawn, this time joined by the trumpeter who'd played "Taps" at the ceremony and they'd involve themselves in a contest to see who could blow the loudest and the most off key. To hear their rendition of "Amazing Grace" was, well, truly amazing.

Incensed neighbors would call out the police force and before long, he'd be joining in the singsong -- along with the neighbors. I don't know how the booze held out. My parents certainly couldn't have afforded to supply it. My guess is that whenever rations got low, someone would pass the hat for funds and they'd select the drunkest among them to drive the 10 miles there and back to the Legion to replenish the stock.

Each of us kids had a secret perch where we could sit unobserved and watch the carryings-on. We'd compare notes in the morning and could have made a fortune out of selling the material to the tabloids or blackmailing the participants if we'd owned a Polaroid.

But the parties took their toll on us youngsters. We'd go to bed wired from the second-hand smoke we'd inhaled, the sips of beer that had been foisted on us by well-meaning celebrants and the high rev brought on by the constant pounding of the piano, adults shouting to be heard and the dim awareness that you weren't witnessing something that normal people usually did.

If you were lucky, you fell asleep right away. Otherwise, you'd hear the party slide into a bear pit of imagined slights, hurt feelings, hurled threats, invitations to step outside, the occasional brawl on the lawn and then a deathly silence as the crowd dissipated into the night.

The mornings after offered the fractured stillness of a worked-over battlefield. The upended lamps would have been righted, the debris from spilled glasses, overflowing ashtrays and broken records cleared away and life would gradually return to normal.

But after some time had elapsed and frayed nerves had had a chance to mend, someone would discover that the Battle of Knackwurst Ridge had occurred on that date and the whole thing would start all over again.

Until I was old enough to know better, I thought there'd been a typographical error made in the Legion motto and that it really should have read: "Lets We Forget". Why else, I reasoned, would normally sane and sensible people -- at least by the standards I'd been exposed to -- go to such lengths to eradicate every last memory of the war years.

CHAPTER NINETEEN
Those Wily Magpies

Mention the word "Magpie Bay" to anyone who has driven through the wilds of Lake Superior country and the response is almost certain to be: "Oh, yeah, that's the place with the statue of the big black and white bird, right?"

There's no geographical reason why Magpie Bay should be better known in the area than, say, Trapper's Cove or Prohibition Run. All three are pleasant little communities offering rest, relaxation and hot and cold running blackflies to the weary motorist.

But Magpie Bay has its Big Bird.

Like the Manneken Pis in Brussels, the Eiffel Tower in Paris and London's Big Ben, the gigantic steel magpie, constructed from iron ore dug out of the surrounding mountains of the Pre-Cambrian Shield, attracts tens of thousands of visitors a year to what would otherwise be a "Welcome To/Thanks For Visiting" blip on the ribbon of concrete that meanders like a drunken badger along the shores of Lake Superior.

The folks in Magpie Bay who make a fair living from the tourists drawn to the town by the big metallic bird owe a large debt of gratitude to a man named Bernie Turcotte. Bernie, so the story goes, was sent into Magpie Bay in 1939 to oversee the installation of new equipment at the Timberline Mine. He apparently fell madly in love with the place (a good choice of adverbs considering what little the area had to offer at the time) and sank his life savings into a clothing store that was up for sale.

Bernie then decided it would be a good idea to wire his family to tell them what he'd done and invite them to join him. Such were his persuasive powers (as we'll see in a moment) that they did, although there's no record of their first comments when they stepped down off the train.

Bernie Turcotte's name figures in just about every wild and crazy scheme the townspeople – who, like the Conchs of Key West, proudly set themselves apart from newcomers by calling themselves Magpies -- came up with over the ensuing 35 years. And there were many of them.

For instance, when the government tried to weasel out of a long-standing promise -- to connect Magpie Bay to Stackton by building a road to augment the rail line and bushplane access -- Bernie was part of the protest committee.

He scoffed at the government's contention that an area of the road allowance called the Eagle Promontory was impenetrable and quickly recruited four young adventurers to walk the 80-mile obstacle course, garnering so much publicity that the government relented.

When a petulant transportation department bureaucrat decided to get even by sending the highway around the town, bypassing the commercial heart of it by more than a mile, Bernie got permission to erect the Big Bird on top of a cairn commemorating the construction of the road link. He then saw to the setting up of an information kiosk near the landmark and began the process of directing thousands of tourists annually off the main highway and into the community.

The only problem here was that, other than the ruins of a frontier fort and Turner's Bowling Alley, which was just about as dilapidated, there weren't many "photo ops" as the volunteer executive director of the Greater Magpie Bay Tourism Authority, who'd taken a mail-order marketing course, used to say.

So Bernie and the boys set out to restore the old fort, building a pioneer village complete with several log huts and a church built of thousands of discarded liquor bottles set in cement. The multi-colored containers created a breathtaking stained glass effect inside the place of worship, which was named, quite appropriately, The Church Of The Departed Spirits.

But the greatest caper those marvelous miscreants of Magpie Bay ever pulled off, in my humble opinion, was the time they came up with a way to shake some of the ill-gotten gains out of the jodhpurs of a certain eccentric English wannabee named Jimmy Dunn.

Sir James, as he liked to be called – although the closest anyone could figure he'd come to being knighted was through a mail-order title he'd purchased in response to an ad in the New York Times -- made his fortune during the pre-Crash 1920s when "business ethics" was even more of a contradiction in terms than it is today.

Anyway, Sir Jimmy, who in later life would have his personal pilot fly to Magpie Bay to pick him some fresh blueberries for dinner at his east coast estate, became interested in the area when he was able to buy the bankrupt steel mills in Stackton for a song during the Depression.

Local mythology has it that Sir Jimmy, apoplectic because the manager of Stackton's one decent hotel wouldn't fire the chef who'd served His Nibs a meal not to his liking, bought the place and fired the offending pot banger.

The nine-story building remained on the steel mills' books for decades until the company could unload it to a couple of local businessmen who ran aground on the financial shoals of the river rapids that ran through Stackton and provided the electrical power to run the mills. After changing hands several times, the once-proud centerpiece of Stackton's downtown commercial area is now a nursing home.

But I digress. Back to Bernie and the boys and the way they took the good Sir James for a ride. It was simple. They hooked him right where the high and mighty have been hooked since the coining of the word "hubris". Right in the old ego.

In 1947, the suggestion was made that the town's name be changed from Magpie Bay to Jamestown in honor of the head of the Stackton steel mills, the company that also owned Timberline

Mine and thus the whole town. The Superior Railroad Line, whose largest customer just happened to be the Stackton mills, coincidentally changed their station name to Jamestown in 1948 and in 1951 the federal post office followed suit.

There followed an avalanche of benevolence from the grateful Baronet, including great lashings of largesse for the Sir James Dunn High School and the Lady Dunn Hospital.

Sir James died in 1956 and by 1960 Jamestown ceased to exist. The townspeople let it be known far and wide that from that day forward their community would answer to the name of Magpie Bay, Land of the Big Black and White Bird.

And they all lived happily ever after.

CHAPTER TWENTY
Free At Last

As I heard it later, Dad decided to tell the big shots at the Timberline Mine where they could shove their timeclock the moment he spotted burning logs floating down the Magpie River.

The Magpie Bay of our time was a tiny community totally surrounded by forested land that the giant lumber companies, like a mutant colony of army ants on a rampage, regularly stripped in ragged sections.

The summer before our forced exile in the northern wilderness ended, lightning or careless loggers or a combination of both started a series of forest fires that eventually ringed the entire town. The bad news was that thick clouds of wood smoke blanketed the whole area. The good news was that the smell of wood smoke blotted out the perpetual smell of sulfur, one of the byproducts of the sintering process that extracted iron ore from rock.

The really bad news, however, was that the firefighters were losing the battle against the multitude of conflagrations that threatened to engulf Magpie Bay and everything in it.

Since the highway link to Stackton hadn't yet been built, there were only two means of exit from that outpost community and back to civilization -- by train or by the small pontoon planes that used Magpie Lake as a runway.

As usually happens in dangerous situations, rumors skittered through the community like rats through a warehouse. The rail line out of town had been buried under tons of rubble by a fire-induced landslide. All the pontoon planes were needed to waterbomb the fires -- and three of them had already crashed. The water tower had been pumped dry by firefighters and we were all going to die of thirst. The last train to make it into Magpie Bay had delivered a shipment of cyanide pills so that we could all commit suicide rather than face the horror of burning to death.

The one rumor the townspeople chose to believe because it offered a frayed lifeline of hope was that the government had begged, borrowed and commandeered float planes from all over North America and they were on their way to Magpie Bay to airlift everybody out.

That uplifting news caused the greatest exodus since a bewigged Charlton Heston took staff in hand and began leading a cast of film extras across the Mojave Desert. People who could walk, ride a bicycle, flag down one of the few vehicles operating at the time or harness a farm animal to a wagon began the trek to Magpie Lake where the air rescue was supposed to take place.

The shores of the lake took on a festive air as people staked out their plot of sand, prepared makeshift beds of clothing and blankets and started fires to cook whatever rations they'd been able to scrounge up in their haste to get away.

Our family, on the other hand, stayed put in our house. My brother and I would make occasional forays down to the beach and bring back intelligence reports to our mother, but no amount of pleading on our part could get her to budge from our home.

"Your father's at the mine and when he decides it's time to move down to the lake, we will," was her unshakeable explanation. "Besides, I don't want him running all over the lakeshore looking for us. I said we'd be here until he came for us and here we'll stay."

What we didn't know at the time, since there were no residential telephones in Magpie Bay to let people keep in touch, was that Dad was frantic with worry. As timekeeper at the mine, he had reports to get out for an upcoming shareholders meeting and while others were leaving their posts to be with their families, he was told that he had to stay on until everything was in order.

From time to time, announcements would come over the loudspeaker in the mine office building that another bus would be leaving shortly to take people home to make preparations for the expected evacuation. Dad kept working at the reports in the hope that he could get them done quickly and be on his way.

At one point, a supervisor walked by and Dad requested permission to pack up and leave.

"We can't have that, old chap," sniffed the departmental manager, who'd spent the Second World War as an officer in the reserves where his worst risk of injury would have been cutting himself on the foil wrapping on a bottle of Johnny Walker Black. "Duty first, that's our motto here."

At that point, so he told us later, Dad saw burning logs floating down the river outside the office window. It was an indication that the fire was getting dangerously close to the town.

But the words: "Duty first" served as the trigger that really set Dad into action. He'd had a bellyful of duty first. He slammed shut the ledger he'd been working on and started putting away the items on his desk, ignoring the protests from his supervisor that he couldn't just up and leave.

Reaching the driveway just as a bus was pulling away, Dad managed to flag it down and arrived at our house in short order. Then, and only then, would our mother agree to gather up as much as we could carry and head for the beach.

The whole thing turned out to be an exercise in futility. There were no planes to evacuate us. That rumor proved to be as reliable as a politician's campaign promises. But it started to rain the morning after we'd set up camp on the beach and we all straggled home to get out of our wet clothes and into a warm bath.

The rain and a shift in the winds extinguished some of the blazes and gave the firefighters a chance to gain control so that the danger eventually passed and things returned to normal.

For everyone but Dad, that is. He became a non-person at work for disobeying an order, as stupid as the order might have been. Fellow office workers, sensing an imminent execution, gave him the cold shoulder in the lunchroom and even after hours. Where our house had been action central for parties and celebrations, hardly anyone came around anymore.

One day one of Dad's bosses suggested they go out for a drink after work. The fellow assured Dad that he was in the doghouse for the moment, but that soon it would all blow over. Then he suggested another drink. And another.

The inevitable happened, as they knew it would. Dad missed work the next day due to a monumental hangover. When he showed up at the mine office the following day, a letter of termination was on his desk. His drinking buddy of two nights before, who had also missed work but had claimed to be a victim of the 24-hour flu, wouldn't even meet his eyes.

Dad made one telephone call from his desk, asking the operator for time and charges and leaving the correct change in a little pile when he left. The call was to a contractor in Stackton whose bacon Dad had saved months before when the man's on-site bookkeeper had skipped town, leaving a payroll to be made up and checks to be issued to workers involved in building a plant extension at the Timberline Mine.

Dad had stayed up all night, sifting through time cards, payroll records and whatever else he could get his hands on. By the time the men started filing into the construction shack for their checks, everything was in order.

The grateful contractor had told Dad then that if he ever needed a job, all he had to do was call. The man was as good as his word and within a few days we were all packed, the keys to the rented house were returned to the landlord and we were on our way back to civilization aboard the Superior Railroad Line.

There were good times ahead for all of us. Dad's drinking problem miraculously cleared up. Not right away. That only happens in the movies. But eventually he became a pillar of the community as an officer of the court in Stackton. He served two terms as president of the regional court association and received accolades from judges, government representatives and civic officials upon his retirement.

Our family over time settled into a routine that included a dog, a car and summers renting a cottage by the lake. The Beverly Hillbillies became the Father-Knows-Best Andersons and peace reigned over the land.

But as time softens the images of days long ago, I think back to those wild and often painful years in a town on the brink of frenzy and, strange as it may seem, I consider myself lucky to have been there.

EPILOGUE

My father died four days short of the 44th anniversary of the 1944 Normandy Invasion. By that time, there were few of his cronies still left to attend his funeral.

But Dick McKinnon led a color party of Legionnaires who stood ramrod straight near Dad's coffin throughout the service, despite the fact that those four old vets were well into their seventies at the time – and the minister droned on interminably.

Just before they closed the coffin, Dick took an artificial poppy from his lapel and pinned it to my father's Legion blazer. Then the color party snapped to attention, gave the coffin a smart salute and marched down the aisle and out of the church. There wasn't a dry eye in the place.

In sifting through Dad's papers a few days after the funeral, I came upon a poem I had written for him a number of years before.

At the time, I had just toured the D-Day beaches in Northern France and had been caught up in a tangle of emotions. Standing on top of an abandoned German gun emplacement, I had gazed down on the coastline where the Allied troops had landed on June 6, 1944.

It was an eerie feeling to know that my father had been one of them and had faced withering machine gun and mortar fire as he and his comrades stormed ashore.

What had really knocked me for a loop was the realization that he had been younger at the time of the Normandy landing than I was on this pilgrimage to the battle site.

Later in the day, I made half a dozen attempts to write him a letter telling him how proud I was of his wartime experiences. Each time, I'd read over what I had set down, then shake my head at the inadequate words, crumple up the notepaper and start again.

I had just about given up hope of ever getting it right when the opening line of a poem popped into my head. I had never written poetry before, but the words flowed from my pen as though someone else was dictating them to me. I got the whole thing down in one take and mailed the poem back home without re-reading it, afraid that I would discard it as I had the aborted letters.

Dad told me later that he cried when he read it.

I would like to dedicate that poem to my father and to all the gallant soldiers who sacrificed their lives for our freedom – some killed in action, others returning home with physical or emotional scars they would carry for the rest of their lives.

THE OLD SOLDIER

Medals – such meager payments for priceless years willingly thrown away –
Are taken from their casual resting place in bureau drawers
And proudly polished to a sheen brass buttons once were given,
Then pinned to coats by hands less steady than when they held a gun.
The faint notes of Reveille can be heard, or are they just imagined?
As a final wipe is given to already gleaming shoes.
The dark blue tam is tugged to a familiar cocky angle
And the old soldiers, downing something to ward off November's chill,
Fall in once more.
The ranks are even thinner this year than each had feared.
A different foe – old age – aided perhaps by too many glasses drained
To numb the painful legacy of war,
Has claimed another score or more of comrades,
Bringing home to those remaining the realization that this might be

Their last parade.
No time for that, the pipes and drums have sounded.
It's effort enough to keep in step on a route that lengthens every year.
Nor is it shortened by the knowledge that the crowd of onlookers
Has also thinned
And some have come to jeer, not pay respects as others did before.
Some of the scoffers, too young to ever have been touched by war,
Snicker when the bugler falters as he plays Taps.
They smirk at each other as the Speaker intones: "Lest we forget."
While a thousand weary eyes regard them sadly
And five hundred hearts whisper: "If you only knew."

●

Printed in the United States
2295